LUCKY DOG

A novel by
Laurie Ezpeleta

Illustrated by
Melissa Glen

This book is dedicated
To the dogs
Who have brightened my days,
And lightened my heart
With their unconditional love.

"The biggest disease this world suffers from
is people feeling unloved."

Princess Diana
1961–1997

CHAPTER ONE

May 1998

"My mom is going to kill me," Emily groaned.

"As she should, young lady." Principal Sweat paused for a moment to peer over wire-rimmed glasses at the girl with the wild red hair and the mismatched outfit. Then she picked up the phone and stabbed at the number pad with the eraser end of a pencil.

Emily sighed loudly and rolled her eyes, then leaned back in the chair and examined a hang-nail on her index finger. She was eager to appear nonchalant although she was listening so hard she could have heard a flea sneeze out on the playground. She felt each jab of the pencil in her gut as if it were a sword plunging between her ribs.

"May I speak with Mrs. Locke?" Tap, tap, tap—the pencil hammered the desk now. "I understand she's busy, but it's important. It's regarding her daughter, Emily." Tap, tap.

Emily felt a lump develop in her throat and risked a furtive glance from under lowered lashes. Tap, tap, tap. The only other person she knew who tapped a pencil like that was her father when he was grading papers. Emily squeezed her eyes shut, took a deep breath and returned her attention to the ragged hangnail. She could feel Principal Sweat looking at her and refused to give her the satisfaction of looking her in the eye.

"Hello, Mrs. Locke? Since Emily is no longer allowed in the after-school program you'll need to come pick her up." Pencil paused...listening. Tap, tap, tap. "I sent a note home with her yesterday for you to sign and return today."

"I forgot to give it to her," Emily muttered. She was not unfamiliar with the room, for although she'd only been at the school for a month, this was not the first time she'd found herself sitting across from the principal. In fact, she had been sitting in this very seat only yesterday. She lowered her lashes, evading Principal Sweat's steely gaze.

"I realize you're busy, but you should check her backpack every day for important papers." Tap, tap, tap. "I'm sorry, but rules are rules. I do understand that this is a difficult time for her, but I have the welfare of others to consider. I wish I could be of more help. I truly am sorry." Tap, tap, tap...faster now. Impatience tinged her voice. "She can either sit in the office and wait for you to get off work or you can come pick her up now." Pause, she listened ...tap, tap, tap, tap, tap. "Yes, the busses have left already. Perhaps a neighbor ...." Tap. "Yes, with your permission she can walk home."

"I thought you're not allowed to say a mother should kill her child," Emily said crossly.

"If you'd paid attention to your English lessons you might have realized that I was speaking figuratively not literally, as were you earlier—at least I assume you didn't *really* mean that your mother was going to kill you."

"Can I go now?"

"Yes Emily, you can go, but I expect you to go straight home. Do you hear me?"

"Yes, Your Majesty," Emily said.

"Are you trying to smart mouth me?"

"Yes, Ma'am, I mean, no Ma'am. Your Majesty is the title for royalty—you know, the people in power. That makes you the queen of our school. That's all."

The principal frowned. "I've heard of your interest in the history of European royalty."

"Yes, Ma'am. Did you know that due to the inbreeding of a common genetic disorder that many of the European royalty were exceptionally ugly."

Principal Sweat's frown deepened and her lips turned down at the corners. "You better go home now, Emily. But that skateboard does not touch the ground until you're off school property. Is that understood?"

CHAPTER TWO

*F*ifteen feet before the edge of school prop-erty, Emily looked back over her shoulder at the red brick building. Satisfied that ol' Principal Sweaty-pants wasn't watching, she dropped her skateboard to the ground and sailed off down the sidewalk towards town singing quietly, "A, B, C, you can't catch me...the cat's got a flea... and the queen's got ta pee...."

The sidewalk ended at the edge of town and the street narrowed into a two-lane highway that circled the lake. Emily's house was on the west side, about two miles down the road and another three blocks up the hill, on a dirt road in the woods. It wasn't really their house. They were just renting it *for the time being*, her mother said. Whatever that means.

Emily could have walked the two miles if she'd wanted but she preferred to ride her skateboard.

The crumbling asphalt at the road's edge was rough and uneven, eroded by years of blanketing winter snows, chains on salted ice and heavy seasonal traffic. She tried to center her board on the white line painted along the side of the road. The paint, a thick fluorescent goo, filled the nooks and crannies providing a smooth surface that was barely wider than her wheels.

Most cars drove around her, giving her a wide berth. Some people honked or rolled down their windows and yelled at her to get out of the street. Others—big scaredy-cats—slowed to a crawl behind her because they were afraid to cross the center divider and afraid to hit her. Emily didn't care. What were they going to do anyway? Run her over? What if they did? Who cares? Maybe she'd get to see her dad again.

A jerk in a Porsche roared by her so closely it nearly blew her off her board. "Get a life!" she yelled. It really wasn't a bad thing to say, she figured, because everybody needed a life. It was certainly better than the alternative.

A big green pick-up passed by her and pulled onto the side of the road. The truck's tires kicked up a blinding cloud of fine gray dust that made her cough and cover her eyes. Jumping off her board, she kicked down on the tail end of it so that it popped up into her left hand, while shielding her face with her right arm. As the dust settled she realized the pick-up was a forest ranger's truck and the forest ranger was headed her way.

"Aren't you the kid who just moved in to the Dew Drop Inn?" he asked.

The ranger was tall, thin and old—even older than her father had been—but beneath the scowl he had kind eyes so she wasn't afraid.

"We've been there over a month now," she said.

"Oh, excuse me," he said dramatically. "Aren't you the kid who moved in to the Dew Drop Inn over a month ago?"

"It's a stupid name for a house," she replied.

The ranger eyed her sternly, walked around to the passenger side of the truck, opened the door, and said, "Get in."

Emily walked up to the Ranger and stared him straight in the eye. She threw her backpack and skateboard in the cab and climbed up into the truck.

They drove for a few minutes in silence, both lost in thought. They passed Crooked Creek. The sparkling stream snaked along the forest floor reflecting an occasional ray of sunlight filtering through the towering cedars and redwoods that stood silent and steady, like the queen's guard. Emily felt a profound loneliness as she stared into the dark and forbidding forest. She shook herself, like a wet dog, to dislodge the feeling.

"You shouldn't be riding that thing in the street, you know." The ranger glanced at her then returned his attention to the road.

Emily laid her hand possessively on her skateboard. Her father had given her the board and her mom said if she broke it or lost it she wasn't getting another one because they were too expensive. "What are you going to do? Arrest me?"

The ranger's expression sharpened. "I might," he said.

"Can rangers actually do that—arrest people?"

"Sure can, we're government officers. But I have more important things to do, so why don't you just stay out of the street?"

Emily sighed and looked out the passenger window.

"And another thing," he added. "You shouldn't get into cars with strangers. Didn't your mother ever tell you that?"

Emily groaned. "You're not a stranger, you're a ranger."

"Just because someone is wearing a uniform doesn't mean you should trust him."

"Just because you're a stranger doesn't mean you're not trustworthy," Emily replied. "Sometimes you just have to have faith and ask for help when you need it."

"Did your mom tell you that?" he asked.

"My dad," she answered. "Where are you taking me anyway?"

"Why to the inn, my lady, the stupidly named, Dew Drop Inn."

They passed the sign for Big Pine and just beyond it the Big Pine Market. "That's where my mom works," Emily said, tapping the window with a grubby finger.

"Is she working now?"

"Yeah, she pretty much works all the time."

"Must be lonely for you."

Emily turned back to the window, her jaw taut.

"If you don't mind," the ranger said, "I need to stop by my office for a second." He pulled into a driveway in front of the log cabin on the corner. In front a wooden sign read, "Big Pine Ranger Station," and below it was a picture of Smokey the Bear and the words, "Only you can prevent forest fires."

"You can wait in the car if you want," he said.

"I didn't know this was your ranger station. I go by here all the time when I walk to the store to see my mom. I live right up the street. Can I come in?" Without waiting for an answer, Emily shoved open the heavy door and jumped down out of the truck. "I always wanted to look inside."

"Sure. I'll show you around. I have some books and maps you might be interested in. Just let me take care of the little guy in back first." The ranger walked to the rear of the truck and opened the tailgate. Leaning into the camper he unhooked a bungee cord and pulled out a medium-sized, plastic animal carrier.

"What is it? Can I see? Can I see?" Emily scrambled to get a peek inside the wire mesh window of the cage.

"Whoa." The ranger laughed and held the carrier out of reach. "Surprise, surprise! You're a kid after all. You were acting so cool I was beginning to think you were a grown-up in disguise."

"I'm not a kid. I'm almost twelve."

"Uhhh, that makes you eleven—a kid in my book."

"Please, let me see!" Emily begged.

"You're not afraid, are you?" the ranger asked.

She shook her head.

"Be very, very careful," he said setting the carrier on the ground in front of her. "And whatever you do, don't stick your fingers in the cage."

Emily's spine tingled with anticipation as she approached the cage. Was it a mountain lion? A porcupine? Maybe a snake?" She knelt down on one knee and peered inside. In the back corner she caught a glimpse of black fluff before it hurled itself at her.

"Arrgh," Emily yelped and fell back on her butt. "What is that?" she cried. "A dog?" She scrambled back onto her feet and stuck her finger in between the wire mesh. "Ouch! He bit me." She watched a bright red bead of blood form on the tip of her finger then she stuck it in her mouth.

"I told you not to stick your finger in the cage," the ranger said.

"Can I hold him?" she asked.

"It's a her. I've got a box set up for her in the corner of my office. You can hold her while I put some paper down and find her some food and water, then I'll take you home."

Emily bent over and carefully unlatched the door to the carrier. Out bounded a small dog with fluffy, black, mottled fur, beady eyes and a sharp, pointed nose. "She's so cute." Emily giggled as the animal climbed into her lap and half way up her chest and started nuzzling and licking her face. She held the squirming mutt out in front of her so she could get a better look. "You

10

are the cutest thing I've ever seen. Who does she belong to?"

"The word is whom—to whom does she belong, and the answer is, no one yet. I'm trying to find her a home. People sometimes come here to the lake and drop off animals they don't want."

"And leave them to die?" Emily asked.

"I think they hope that someone will take them and give them a good home."

"Can I have her? I'll give her a good home."

"What?" The ranger stopped what he was doing, crossed his arms, cocked an eyebrow and looked at her sternly. "Well, I don't know. What would your parents say?"

"It's just my mom. My dad doesn't live with us any more. But she wouldn't care. In fact, she'd love to have a dog—we've been looking for one." Emily crossed the fingers of the hand that was buried in black fur and hoped that God wouldn't strike her dead.

"You never told me your name," the ranger said.

"Emily."

"Well, you wouldn't lie to me now, Emily, would you?"

Emily crossed the fingers on her other hand and then crossed her legs for good measure. "Cross my heart, hope to die, stick a needle in my eye."

"No need to do that. I just don't want your mom to be upset with me."

"Oh, no sir, she won't."

"Okay then, Emily. Hop back in the truck and I'll drive you and your new friend home."

Emily climbed back into the truck holding the eager little dog in her arms. She grinned and buried her face in soft fur as the ranger closed her door and walked around to the driver's side of the cab. She giggled as the dog nipped at her nose and licked her ears.

As the ranger drove her home he quizzed Emily on her new responsibilities.

"I promise I'll remember to walk, feed, brush, and bathe her"—she frowned for a moment—"oh yeah, and give her fresh water every day. I promise I'll take the best care of her—I'll be the best dog-care-er person ever. Hey," she said, as they pulled into the dirt driveway in front of her cabin, "what's her name?"

"She's your dog, you tell me," the ranger said.

"I don't know."

"When you look at her what comes to mind?"

"Luck. I feel like the luckiest person in the whole world."

"Then you should name her Lucky. Now go on, get inside and see if Lucky needs a drink of water." The ranger opened her door and helped her down from the truck with her armload of precious cargo. Then he carried her skateboard and backpack to the front porch.

"Thank you," Emily said, shifting the dog to her hip so she could get the house key hidden in a pot of pansies on the front deck. "Thank you for the ride and for Lucky and...uh...just thank you for everything, Ranger Stranger."

The ranger cocked his head and smiled. "You and Lucky come around and see me sometime." He climbed back in his truck and drove off kicking up a billowing cloud of dust behind him.

"Mom is really going to kill me this time," Emily said to the squirming dog as she unlocked the front door. "And I mean literally, not figuratively."

CHAPTER THREE

Emily Mary Locke, if you don't get your bum out of bed right now, you'll be late for school."

Emily dropped the heating pad and took a swig from the steaming thermos. Pulling her robe snugly around her, she tied the sash and walked into the kitchen. Her mother was standing over the sink eating cereal.

"Hurry up, honey, I have to be at work early this morning," her mother mumbled through a mouthful of granola. Setting the bowl in the sink, Diana Locke turned to look at her daughter. "What's the matter with you? Why aren't you dressed yet?"

"I don't feel so good," Emily said. She placed both hands on her belly for emphasis.

"What? You don't look...." Emily's mother laid her hand on her daughter's forehead. "You're burning up. Let me get the thermometer."

Emily groaned dramatically and plopped down on a kitchen chair.

Her mother returned and stuck the thermometer in Emily's mouth. "You know the routine— under your tongue with your mouth shut for two minutes."

Emily clamped her lips around the glass rod and nodded.

"Did you hear anything strange last night?" her mother asked, while she kept an eye on the second hand of her watch. "When I went to bed I thought I heard whining and scratching noises like there was a small animal under the house—a raccoon or something."

Emily shook her head and shrugged her shoulders.

"You don't think wild animals could be getting into the yard or nesting under the house, do you?" her mother asked. "Don't answer that. Don't open your mouth. Time's not up yet," she said, tapping the face of her watch.

Finally Diana took the thermometer from Emily's mouth and held it up in front of her nose to read. "One hundred and one! Looks like you're not going anywhere today, young lady. Back to bed! I better call Mr. Johnson at the store and let him know that I can't come in today."

"No," Emily yelped. "Mr. Johnson needs you, and...I'm a big girl. I can stay home by myself."

"But—" Diana looked doubtfully at her daughter.

"Really, Mom. I'm almost twelve. You're going to have to leave me alone sometime."

Diana sighed. "Maybe you're right." She caressed her daughter's cheek. "You've practically grown-up over night."

Emily noticed tears suddenly fill her mother's eyes—as they did so often these days—and looked away.

"I'll tell Mr. Johnson I need to come home at my lunch break to check on you," Diana said, reaching for her purse and keys. "I'll bring you something special to eat."

"Thanks, Mom," Emily said.

"Let me tuck you into bed before I go."

"No!"

"What?"

"I mean...uh...you don't have to. I'm a big girl. Remember?"

"Well, you'll always be my little girl. Now jump into bed and I'll bring you a glass of orange juice."

Emily climbed into her bed and pulled the covers up to her chin.

Her mother opened the door. "It's dark in here," she said.

"Don't turn on the lights. I'm trying to sleep."

"Okay, honey." Tiptoeing in, she set the glass down on the bedside table. "Here's your orange juice," she whispered.

"Thanks, Mom. Have a good day."

Diana sat down on the edge of the bed to kiss Emily on the forehead. When the lump she thought was tangled bedclothes moved, she screamed and leapt so high that she nearly hit her head on the ceiling.

"What is that?" Diana shrieked. She switched on the lamp and stared in horror, her eyes round as pizzas, at the wriggling lump under the quilt. Reaching for the covers with a trembling hand, she wrestled them loose from Emily's iron grip and yanked them back.

Lucky jumped up, to greet Emily's mom like a Jack in the Box. Diana screamed.

Emily grabbed the dog and held her tight. Lucky wriggled and writhed, trying to break free. That night Emily had hidden her under the back porch. Later she had heard her whining and scratching to get out. She had hoped and prayed that her mother wouldn't notice over the noise from the TV. After her mother had cried herself to sleep on the couch, an empty wine bottle on the floor beside her, Emily brought the squirming pup into her bed hoping she'd settle down for the night. It had worked—until now.

"Mom! It's okay!" Emily had to yell to be heard over her mother's hollering.

"Geez! What is that?" Diana screeched. "A raccoon?" She was on the verge of hysteria.

"She's my dog, Mom. Her name is Lucky. Do you like her?" Emily asked hopefully. She held the dog up for her mom to see.

Her mom looked stunned. Holding a hand over her heart and breathing heavily, Diana said, "That is the ugliest dog I have ever seen!" Suddenly her eyes narrowed as she gathered her senses. "What do you mean *your* dog?"

"She's mine." Emily clutched Lucky in her arms. "The ranger gave her to me."

"The ranger? When? What are you talking about?"

"The ranger said I should have her, because she needed a good home, and because she might even die if nobody wanted her."

"The ranger said that?"

"Yeah...well...that's pretty much what he said."

"Pretty much...?" Diana's eyes hardened as she took in the electric heating pad and the thermos that were stashed between the bedside table and the bed.

Emily could practically see the wheels going round and round in her mom's head, getting hotter and hotter by the second. Her expression was explosive, like she'd been hit in the face with a red paint ball. Emily sunk lower in her bed, and waited for the sky to fall.

When her mom finally spoke, her voice was velvet but her tone was barbed wire. "You have two minutes. Get dressed for school and get in the car. I'll be waiting."

"Yes, Mom."

"And don't forget to bring that animal," she said, walking out the door and shutting it firmly behind her.

Emily had a hard time opening the car door with both the dog and her backpack in her arms, but her mother made no move to help her. In fact, she just stared forward through the windshield as if Emily weren't even there. Emily had never seen her mom like this. It made her stomach twist in pain and for a moment she was glad that she didn't have any breakfast. She was really scared.

"What are you going to do?" Emily asked after she finally got herself settled in the passenger seat.

Diana shifted the car into gear and started driving down the hill without saying a word. When she reached the ranger station she pulled in and parked.

Emily noticed that the ranger's truck was parked at the side of the building and the sign in the window said, "OPEN".

"No Mom, please...." Emily hugged Lucky so tight the little dog yelped.

The door to the station opened and Ranger Stranger trotted down the steps to greet them. Emily's mom leapt out of her car. The ranger's smile froze on his face when he saw her expression.

"How dare you," her mom said angrily.

"No, Mom, no!" Emily cried. "It's not his fault. I lied to him. I told him we wanted a dog."

"You what?" Diana turned on her daughter.

Emily's tummy felt squirrelly enough to blow chunks. "I'm sorry, Mom. I shouldn't have lied, but I wanted her so much. I need Lucky." Emily nuzzled the dog who licked her neck and chin. "And Lucky needs me."

"I'm sorry, Ms...." The ranger stepped forward.

"Locke, Diana Locke."

"I'm sorry, Ms. Locke. " The ranger took Lucky from Emily's arms, "Sorry to have caused you any trouble. No problem though. I heard that there are some people down in Barron's Bay who are looking for a dog."

Emily gasped, "Barron's Bay—but that's so far." Her voice quivered but she refused to let them see her cry. "I won't even be able to visit her."

"I'm sorry it didn't work out for you, Emily, but you can be happy for Lucky. They are a nice family and they'll give her a good home."

"Thank you for being so understanding," Diana said stiffly. "And I apologize for my daughter's behavior. I promise, she will be punished."

The ranger looked at Emily for what felt like forever.

He turned to her mom and said, "I've got a backroom that needs cleaning. Maybe that can be her punishment."

Diana looked from the ranger to Emily and back again. "Well, I don't know," she said.

"I could use the help," he said. "And it would give her something to do after school. I gather she's not going to the after-school program any more."

"Well—" Diana weighed her options, "—all right."

"Then it's settled," the ranger said. He turned to Emily, "And you—I'll be looking for you on the bus after school today. The bus—no skateboarding."

Emily saluted. "Yes sir, Ranger Stranger."

"Emily!" Her mom said.

Emily wasn't sure whether her mother looked more horrified or embarrassed. But she was sure she was in even more trouble now than she was

21

before. She didn't care. She was really mad at her mom—really, really mad. In fact, her mom was the meanest mother in the whole world. Emily wasn't sure she'd ever be able to forgive her mom for making her give back Lucky.

"It's okay, Ms. Locke. It's a little joke between Emily and me." He smiled but Emily just looked down at her feet. "My real name is Wade Carson."

"Well, thank you, Ranger Carson." Diana smiled weakly and stuck out a hand.

"Call me Wade."

"Wade, then." Diana shook his hand and turned to Emily. "Now get in the car, Emily. You're late for school and I'm even more late for work."

Emily did as she was told. Diana peeled out of the driveway at an alarming rate of speed, but Emily hardly noticed. Her eyes were glued to Lucky squirming in the Ranger's arms and her heart was breaking.

CHAPTER FOUR

"Emily Mary Locke! Did you hear me? I said, get out of bed this minute."

Emily rolled over and pulled the covers over her head. She wasn't getting up now, and as far as she was concerned, she wasn't getting up ever again. Yesterday had been the worst day of her life. First Mom made her give Lucky back to the ranger. Then she got sent to Queen Sweaty-pants' office *again* for having her head down on the desk and refusing to do her work, or participate in class—she was too depressed! Then the kids on the bus made fun of her. They called her, "Emily, the Strange," who is actually a little dark haired girl with a black cat. She's not even real—she's just a character on a sticker Emily's father had given her a long time ago when he bought her the skateboard. Dad had said it reminded him of her—which she liked until now that the kids had started using it against her.

Emily had asked, "But, Dad, why does she remind you of me? Is it because we're both named Emily?"

He just looked at her and smiled. It was the grin he wore when he expected her to do the thinking, to put the pieces together and come up with the answer.

"Because I don't look a bit like her, Dad. I don't have straight black hair or bangs, and I don't have a cat. I don't even like cats."

Her father was still grinning.

"Oh, I get it," Emily said. "You think I'm strange like her? Thanks a lot! What kind of a dad are you?"

"Strange isn't necessarily a bad thing, Emily. Technically it only means *different*. In this world it's not so bad to be different. It just means you do things your way, no matter what anyone else says. Your namesake was strange in that way too—a good way."

Emily knew she was named after Emily Bronte, the nineteenth century writer. Her dad swore that he'd intended on naming her that even before she was born and it was just a coincidence that they were both born on July 30th—but it was kind of a mystic coincidence just the same. It was, in fact, the same type of coincidence that brought her parents, Charles and Diana, together and saw them married the same year as the royal couple with the same names.

"What did she do?" Emily had asked her dad.

"Well...." Her dad drummed his fingers on his desk as he searched for the right words. "Emily Bronte was quite a strange little girl too—she created her own fantasy world named Gondal that was ruled by a woman who was always in control of herself and her life, which was rather unusual for the times. And then, as an adult, Emily wrote *Wuthering Heights*, which was condemned for being shocking—which of course meant that everybody was dying to read it. When they did people decided it was obviously written by a man, because it was much too coarse and intense and violent for a woman to have written. So you see, she was quite the independent thinker—just like you."

Emily thought about it for a while and then decided she liked her name. "So was Emily Bronte's middle name Mary, too?" She asked.

"No, it was Jane."

"So who was Mary? Not the one who said, 'Let them eat cake,' was she?"

"No, no, no—that was Marie. I'd never name you after a cream puff like that. Your middle name, Mary, is for Mary Stuart—Queen of Scots. But I don't have time to tell you about her now. I've got papers to grade. We'll save that story for another day."

"Emily!"

Her mother's voice snapped Emily back to the present like a rubber band that had stretched back to the past and then released.

Sticking her head in the door, her mother insisted, "Get up now! I need to go to the store."

"No. Go away. I hate you." Emily rolled over to face the wall.

"Is this because of that dog?"

"Lucky was my dog. The ranger gave her to me. You had no right to take her away."

"I'm your mother. I have every right."

"Dad would have let me keep her."

"Well, Dad's not here any more. It's just you and me now. Forever!"

"I wish...I wish...."

"What? That I'd died instead of Dad? Is that what you wish?" Her mother's eyes flashed.

Fighting back tears, Emily glared at her mother. Her lower lip trembled.

"Well you know what, Emily? Sometimes I wish I had died instead of him too." Her Mother's anger collapsed and she buried her head in her hands, frustrated by the tears that flowed so easily these days. "I can't do it alone. I just can't. It's too hard. I miss him so much. It should have been me, not him."

"Stop crying, Mom. It's all right. I'm sorry." Emily hated to see her mom cry and she hated herself for making her cry. She hated admitting that sometimes she felt that very thing. When Princess Diana died everyone secretly wished it had been Prince Charles because nobody liked him much. And when Charles Locke died, well... it's not that people didn't like Diana Locke, just that everybody *loved* Charles Locke. Over four hundred people attended his funeral.

Her mother hadn't stopped crying since then. Soon she started drinking and some days she didn't even get out of bed unless she had to go to work.

Emily knew her mom only needed to go to the store this morning because she wanted to buy more booze. She brought groceries home from the little market she worked at. But she didn't want her boss to know she drank, so she was going to drive all the way to the supermarket on the far side of Emerald Lake, where no one knew her, to buy her zombie potion.

Emily rubbed her mother's back. It was as if she didn't know Emily was there. Her mother sunk into funks where she hardly acknowledged Emily at all. On those days Emily felt invisible. The rest of the time Emily felt like an annoyance—a sliver of glass in her mother's foot or a mosquito buzzing her head.

Emily was certain her dad wouldn't have abandoned her as her mother had—her mother was acting like Emily didn't exist, like she'd died too. But she was still a solid, living breathing, *visible* person. It was as if her mom wanted to dive into that grave with her dad, and didn't care that she was leaving Emily all alone to fend for herself.

"I'll make you a cup of tea, Mom. It'll make you feel better."

"No, I have to go to the store. I want you up though, to watch for the mailman. I'm expecting a Social Security check today. You know I hate to leave them sitting in the box. Can't afford to have one stolen."

Emily got up and looked for something to wear. She picked up the shorts and tee shirt, she'd worn the day before, from the floor and held them up. They were clean when she went to school yesterday but had gotten pretty grubby when she cleaned the dusty, old backroom at the ranger station. She shrugged and put them on. It had been a long time since her mom had taken her shopping. Fewer and fewer of the clothes in her drawers fit her any more and the ones that did, didn't match. The last time Emily had mentioned it to her mother, Diana had given her a blank look and then taken another sip from her glass.

"Okay Mom, you can go now," Emily said, walking into the kitchen. She opened the refrigerator door and peered inside.

"I won't be long." Her mom picked up her purse and keys and lowered dark sunglasses over red-rimmed eyes. "Don't forget...."

"I won't forget the stupid check in the mail," Emily said, pulling out a carton of milk and sniffing it suspiciously. Everything was about money these days. Money, money, money! Her dad had life insurance when he died, but it was gone. Mom said they had to pay 20 percent of the hospital bill and 20 percent of a lot is still *a lot*. Her mom was a nurse at the hospital, but after Dad died she didn't go back. Said she couldn't face any more death and dying so she just up and quit. Then she couldn't face seeing Dad's empty chair at the kitchen table, Dad's empty recliner in the den, or his empty desk in the office that still had stacks of papers and books on it collecting dust. So she packed up, rented out the house for a year, and moved them both to Emerald Lake, where they rented a cabin with a silly name from the aunt of a friend from the hospital where she used to work. *I mean, who names a cabin The Dew Drop Inn? Ugh.*

Diana opened the front door, stepped out and screamed. She stumbled back into the cabin as a fluff of black fur, yipping with joy, jumped up to greet her.

"Lucky!" Emily shouted. She knelt down to greet her dog.

CHAPTER FIVE

"Well, I'll be." The ranger scratched his head and looked down at Lucky who was happily snuggled in Emily's arms. "That little dog sure walked a long way to get back to you. I wouldn't have thought she could make it that far. She must have walked all night long."

"So you'll take her back to the people in Barron's Bay?" Diana said. She tapped her foot impatiently and glanced at her wristwatch.

"Well now, I spoke with them this morning and they're not sure they want her back. Said they had her fenced in their yard last night and they don't have a clue how she escaped. They don't think they can keep a dog who can break out of their yard like that."

"What are you going to do?" Diana's voice was sharp.

Emily looked back and forth between her mother and the ranger. She couldn't believe she was about to lose Lucky all over again. Twice in two days was more than a person could bear.

"It seems to me Lucky has made her decision," the ranger said.

Diana's jaw dropped. "What?"

"And if I may be frank, Mrs. Locke, it seems to me this little girl of yours could use a dog."

"But...we can't afford a dog."

"I do apologize, but if it's about the money, I happen to be friends with Doc Soleil, our veterinarian. He's over there on First Street, a block up from the post office. Maybe I can talk to him about a discount on shots and things, seeing as how you would be helping out the community by taking this little fellow in." He scratched Lucky under the chin. "And, the market must get torn bags and dented cans of dog food. I'm sure Pete Johnson would sell them to you at a discount."

"But...but...."

"And old Mrs. Stevens, your landlady, won't mind. She always kept a dog at the Dew Drop Inn. It's fenced and has a nice little doggie door into the back porch for cold nights."

"Can we keep her, Mom? Please."

Diana ran a hand through her long auburn hair and shook her head.

"Please, Mom. I'll take real good care of her, I promise. You'll hardly know she's around."

"I don't know, Emily. A dog is a big commitment."

"You ladies might feel a little safer with a watch dog on duty." The ranger winked at Emily.

She realized she had found a friend in him.

"School will be out this week," he continued. "It would be nice for Emily to have company this summer while you're at work."

"Oh, all right." Diana was exasperated at being outnumbered. "We'll give it a try for a couple of weeks and see how it goes. But if I say Lucky goes after that, then she goes, without an argument from either of you."

"It's a deal." Emily said, grinning from ear to ear.

"A deal," echoed the Ranger. "I'll personally take the responsibility of finding Lucky a new home if it doesn't work out."

CHAPTER SIX

Emily stood waist high in the marsh grasses when her stomach growled. She was hungry. She looked up at the sky. Its brilliance had dimmed as the sun dropped behind the mountaintops and dusk settled around her. She'd better get going if she wants to make it home before dark. Her mother was working so it wasn't that she was going to get in trouble for being late or anything, but the woods could get darker than your darkest nightmares at night unless a full moon happened to be watching over you.

Lucky was by her side, nearly hidden by the tall grasses. The dog stood on her short little legs and wagged her bushy tail expectantly.

"We'd better get going, girl. Just let me throw back this tadpole." Emily held up a small plastic container and examined the gray, fat-headed, skinny tailed, amphibian swimming in a couple of inches of water. One side of the container was magnified allowing Emily to look closely at any creatures she found. It was a gift from Ranger Stranger after she spent an afternoon helping him restock shelves at the station. He gave it to her on one condition, that she releases everything she catches back into the wild.

"Or maybe it's a pollywog," she continued talking to the dog, Kneeling down, she said, "I don't really know the difference. I'll have to ask the ranger. Maybe he has a book at the station. I can look it up." She poured the container's contents back into the narrow creek and watched it, with a swish of its tail, join other froglings in the shadows, where the over-hanging vegetation afforded some protection, and the growth of algae provided food.

She walked towards the road, carefully choosing each step. The meadow was criss-crossed with narrow, shallow tributaries that carried snowmelt run-off from the mountain peaks to the glacial valley that was Emerald Lake. In the tall grass it was easy to step down into one of the creeks without seeing it first. The drop was always a jolt. The icy water flooding her good skate shoes was even worse, not to mention the irritation of squishing with every step thereafter. The spired tips of golden rod and delicate, umbrella shaped, Queen Ann's Lace rustled as Lucky picked her way alongside Emily in, what was for her, a towering forest of undergrowth.

Suddenly Lucky growled and barked sharply.

"What?" Emily started to say when she heard buzzing and noticed the nest she had just disturbed with her foot. The buzzing grew louder as angry bees sounded the alarm.

Emily didn't wait to see them gather forces and rise against her. She started running as fast as she could. "Come on, Lucky," she shouted.

Emily could hear Lucky scrambling through the tall grass behind her. The dog barked a few times. It sounded like she turned to circle back into the marsh. Lucky was drawing the swarm away from Emily. Emily listened intently, her eyes straining in the twilight. Satisfied the bees were no longer chasing her, she plunked down on a fallen log on the side of the road.

Minutes later the dog emerged from the undergrowth and let out a yelp of pain. Emily ran to her. Using the lid of her Creature Container, she flicked a yellow jacket off the dog's nose, two off her back and swatted at a few more with her hand.

"Whew, that was a close call," she said.

Lucky wagged her tail, whined and rested her head on Emily's knee.

"Son of a Slitheren," Emily cried, looking closely at the dog's face. "Your nose is swollen from a bee sting. Oh, poor Lucky." Emily lifted the small dog into her arms and held her close. "My poor, poor Lucky dog. We better go home and put some ice on it."

Suddenly a shadow swooped down from the sky. A shade darker than the deepening sky it took a moment to register in Emily's brain. Bats. Searching the darkness she recognized several of them soaring above her using their radar to find and dine on the mosquitoes, gnats and other insects that emerged at dusk.

"Let's get out of here, Lucky. It's getting dark really fast." Emily climbed on her skateboard and using her left foot to propel herself, took off towards home with Lucky at her heels. She reached the top of the hill and pushed off one more time with her back leg. Experience had taught her if she pushed hard enough at the top of the hill she could make it all the way down and almost to her front door without having to push again.

The road was rough and uneven. She could feel a steady vibration throughout her body that made her nose itch. She reached up to scratch her nose. Suddenly the board stopped short beneath her feet and she flew forward. One of her dad's graduate students, Daryl—an awesome skater—had taught her to tuck and roll when she fell. It was a lesson she never forgot. She curled into a ball and rolled when she hit the road, just as Daryl taught her. She rolled off the pavement onto the gravel roadside and down a grassy culvert before landing heavily on her back in a few inches of water.

Instantly, Lucky was by her side licking her face.

"It's all right, girl." Emily conducted a mental check for injury. She wiggled her toes and flexed her fingers. She sat up, plucked a piece of gravel from her knee and watched a drop of blood form and then ooze down her leg. Other than having the wind knocked out of her, the worst damage was to her clothes. She needed to get home. She was cold and wet, but also she knew that if her mother caught her in these clothes she'd figure out what happened and yell at her for not wearing a helmet.

As Emily started to get up she heard a hissing sound and froze. Looking around slowly she found herself within spitting distance of an angry mother skunk and her kits.

Being nocturnal, they had just come out for the evening when they were rudely interrupted by Emily's sudden arrival. The mother skunk hissed and stomped her feet, her stripped tail held high. Then she turned her rear end towards Emily.

Lucky, leaped across the ditch, barking wildly.

"Lucky!" Emily watched the skunk take aim and release a shower of oily, fetid, stench at the dog.

Lucky yelped and immediately started rubbing her fur along the grassy slope while Cruella DeVil and her kits beat a hasty retreat back in the direction they had come.

"Lucky!" Emily cried. "You saved me again." She knelt down to pick up her dog but quickly changed her mind. "You stink!" Lucky reeked of rotten eggs mixed up with even grosser stuff than that. Emily couldn't bring herself to touch her. Covering her nose with her hand, Emily started breathing out of her mouth. "Come on, Lucky. We need to find you some help."

CHAPTER SEVEN

Dr. Ben Soleil sat hunched over paperwork at his desk. His office manager, Missy, was on vacation, and his veterinary assistant, Karen—who was so pregnant she had no ankles and couldn't see her feet—had cut back her hours. He needed to find more help, but first he needed to pay the bills and update his books.

His stomach growled and he considered ordering a pizza. Perhaps he would be done with the paperwork by the time it arrived. His mouth watered as he considered toppings. Pepperoni. Mushrooms. Maybe he would order the works— a big one because he was hungry, really hungry.

A light knock at the door brought him back to the moment. He groaned. All he needed was an emergency. He'd never finish his books.

Dr. Soleil unlocked the deadbolt and opened the front door to his veterinary clinic. Assaulted by the unmistakable odor of skunk, he covered his nose and looked for the culprit.

The porch light illuminated a young girl. Her elbows and knees were scraped and streaked with drying blood and her clothes were torn and muddy. A pathetic looking mutt stood at her side—the culprit! "Hold on there," he ordered, raising his hand to prevent them from getting any closer.

"Sorry to bother you," the girl said, "but do you have any tomato juice? Maybe some V8 or Bloody Mary mix?" She had dirt on her cheek and pine needles stuck in her hair. "That's what you're supposed to use for skunks. Isn't it?"

"Take your dog around back. There's an old bathtub back there. Put the dog in it and I'll be there in a minute." Dr. Soleil frowned as he shut the door and locked it again. Walking towards the supply closet near the back of his clinic, he pulled his cell phone from his pocket and pushed the button for Pete's Pizza, which he kept on speed dial like a true bachelor.

The sky was pitch black now but Emily and Lucky set off motion lights along the cedar-sided building as they followed the walkway towards the back of the clinic. When she turned the corner it miraculously lit up bright as day and they found a claw-footed, porcelain tub on the rear deck. It had a drain and a hand-held sprayer and everything just like a real, honest to goodness, indoor tub. Emily tried to imagine taking a bath in it—outside, in front of God and everybody—but couldn't. Even the thought made her feel vulnerable and she hated that feeling more than any other.

Getting Lucky into the tub was harder than she thought. In the first place, she didn't want to touch Lucky's fur where it was slick with skunk slime. Even getting near Lucky made her eyes sting and her stomach turn. She pulled the neck of her tee-shirt up over her nose but it didn't help, the smell permeated everything. Using paper towels she found on a shelf near the door, she picked up the dog and holding her at arms length dumped her into the tub. Lucky whined and looked at her with sad, moist eyes.

The vet came out of the back door carrying a plastic tub with some stuff in it that didn't look a thing like tomato juice. Emily looked at him, pulled her shirt down off her nose, and raised her eyebrows questioningly.

"Tomato juice doesn't work. It's an old wives' tale," he said. "It just covers the smell. You need to eliminate the smell with a chemical reaction."

Emily nodded. "You know, in the old days people used perfume to cover up their body odor instead of taking a bath."

Dr. Soleil was surprised this disheveled little girl would make a connection between tomato juice and perfume. She was smart. What was she doing out alone after dark? She obviously had some kind of accident. Where was her mother? He set down the container and started adding the ingredients.

She stepped up to watch. "What are you doing?"

"Mix a quart of hydrogen peroxide with baking soda and liquid soap," he explained, as he performed the task in front of her. "The hydrogen peroxide reacts with the baking soda to make oxygen. The oxygen ties up the 'stink' molecules, then the soap separates them from your dog." He looked to see if the girl understood.

She smiled and nodded.

"What's your dog's name?"

"Lucky."

"And what happened to her nose?" Dr. Soleil asked, noticing the poor mutt's swollen snout.

"She got stung by a bee."

"She got sprayed by a skunk and stung by a bee all in one day? That doesn't sound very lucky to me."

"Yeah, I know." Emily nodded thoughtfully. "I think I'm more lucky to have her than she is to have me." Remembering her manners, she said, "Oh, and I'm Emily. Emily Locke."

So *this* was the little girl the ranger, Wade Carson, told him about. He could see why Wade had taken an interest in her.

"Here." He handed Emily the sponge. "Give Lucky a good scrubbing with this stuff and then rinse her off real well. I'll go inside and get some towels."

Dr. Soleil returned a few minutes later with towels as Emily was rinsing Lucky.

"You know," she said, as she turned off the water and reached for a towel, "King Louis XIV only took three baths in his lifetime."

"Ugh." Dr. Soleil grimaced.

"Yes, pretty gross, huh? And when Queen Victoria moved into Buckingham Palace in 1837—it didn't have one single bathroom."

"How do you know all this?" the vet asked.

"Oh, I know lots of things. Mary, Queen of Scots—I was named after her—she loved to take baths. Had her own bathhouse built at Holyrood Palace. Everyone thought she was crazy. I got to see it when I was there last summer."

"I thought your name was Emily."

She grinned. "My middle name is Mary." She wrapped Lucky in a towel and lifted her from the tub. "And," she continued, "Queen Mary loved dogs—just like I do."

"All right, Queen Mary, let's get Lucky inside and under a dryer and maybe you would like to clean up yourself. There's a shower in the bathroom on the left. Let me get a towel and some clean scrubs for you to put on, and a plastic bag to put those wet stinky clothes in."

"Okay," Emily said. Suddenly she was dying to wash the dirt off.

"And give me a number where I can reach your mom to come pick you up."

"You don't need to do that," Emily assured him. She knew if her mom found out about this she would be mad at her for causing trouble again.

"Yes, Emily, I do. Don't worry. I'll explain it all to her. She works at the store, doesn't she?"

Emily nodded glumly.

"Is she working tonight?" When Emily nodded again Dr. Soleil said he'd call immediately. "Now hurry up with that shower."

Emily stood under the hot water and rinsed the day's dirt from her body. She washed her hair with shampoo she found on the shelf and dried with a soft fluffy towel. The green scrubs the vet had given her were huge. She put on the shirt and it hung down to her knees. Luckily the pants had a drawstring or they would never have stayed up. She had to roll the cuffs up several times before she could walk in them.

The aroma of fresh pizza made her stomach growl so loudly that she feared Dr. Soleil could hear it all the way down the hall. She found him sitting at a table in the small break room. It had a refrigerator, hotplate and microwave oven that shared counter space with an assortment of medical instruments and machines. The pizza was huge and smothered with everything. It wasn't exactly her favorite, because her favorite was sausage and black olive, but she didn't care because she was hungry enough to eat the whole thing herself. Her mouth started to water and she could practically taste it. But she hadn't been invited and she had enough pride not to invite herself. She'd already taken enough of the vet's time. He'd been nicer than she had a right to expect.

Ben Soleil savored the rich tangy tomato sauce, the grilled vegetables, the spicy sausage and pepperoni, and the velvety smooth texture of the melted cheese. He was in heaven. Emily walked in, her wet hair dripping down her back. She looked like a waif in his green scrub's, which hung from her like a tent. He eyes were glued to the pizza.

"So, how much do I owe you?" she asked.

"Here." He handed her a paper plate. "Dig in."

"Really?" Emily said.

"I ordered extra just for you," he said with a wink. "I hate to eat alone."

He didn't have to ask twice. Emily reached for a slice of pizza and devoured it so quickly he was afraid she'd choke. Then she looked up at him tentatively with those big, green eyes.

"Go ahead, have another," he offered.

She rewarded him with a giant toothy grin. This time she ate slowly, pausing to pepper him with questions about being a vet—a job, she considered, to be the best in the whole wide world. When she finished the slice she again asked about his fees.

"I don't know, Emily. How much money do you have?" His eyes twinkled until Emily's face collapsed.

"I have seven dollars and forty-seven cents in a jar under my bed," she said. "It's mostly quarters and pennies. I know it's not enough. Maybe I could help out around here like I did at the ranger station."

"Humm." The vet chewed while he considered her offer.

Emily leaned back and rubbed her belly. She was stuffed. When they heard a knock at the door, she groaned. It had to be her mother.

"Traitor," she grumbled, as Dr. Soleil got up to answer the door.

"Emily Mary Locke!" Diana stormed into the break room. She only called Emily by all three of her names when she was mad. "What have you gotten yourself into now?" Diana looked tired. She ran her hand through her hair, which she only did when she was frustrated. "And what happened to your clothes?"

Emily looked down at the green scrubs. "Mom! I didn't do anything. Lucky got sprayed by a skunk...and I...I mean we...cleaned her up and then I showered...and, uh...well, Dr. Soleil let me borrow these."

"You might want to burn her clothes," the vet said. "I don't think they're salvageable."

Emily's mother glared at him. He quit talking and she turned back to her daughter. "Fine. Just fine!" she said. "How am I supposed to pay for a vet visit—after hours no less?"

"Please, Mrs. Locke. It's okay. Would you like a slice of pizza?" Dr. Soleil offered her a paper plate.

"Pizza?" Diana looked at Dr. Soleil like he'd grown two heads.

"I'm going to pay for it, Mom," Emily said

"You?" Her mother's voice was shrill.

"My office lady is on vacation," Doc Soleil said.

"He needs someone around here to help answer the phones and sweep up and stuff. The ranger told him what a good job I did at the station." Emily smiled proudly.

Her mother looked doubtful.

"Please Mom, it's just for a while—until his office lady comes back."

"I am in a jam," the vet admitted.

"Emily, what am I going to do with you?" Diana ran her fingers through her hair again. "Okay. Okay!" Taking a deep breath, and letting it out slowly, she reached for a slice of the pizza.

CHAPTER EIGHT

Emily settled into a summer routine. Every morning, after completing her chores, she and Lucky visited either the ranger or Dr. Soleil to see if they needed help. She liked the way they treated her like a grown-up, and she loved the money she was paid for the odd jobs she did.

She had helped out in Dr. Soleil's office for nearly two weeks to pay her debt. She was buying her own dog food and had even paid for Lucky's shots and a check-up with the money she made. The doc gave her an employee discount of twenty-five percent, which he showed her how to figure on the calculator. She learned how to answer the phones, fill out the appointment book, and dig out files from the cabinets on the animals that were due that day. She learned how to weigh the animals and record their weights on their charts. She swept the floors, took out the trash, dusted and straightened magazines in the waiting room every afternoon. But her favorite job of all was feeding and walking the animals that were boarding at the clinic while their owners were away.

Her mom was still working a lot at the Big Pine Market. Still drinking and crying herself to sleep pretty much every night. But on the whole they were getting along better. Her mom was no longer saying, "Quit bothering those people. Don't be a pest. They have work to do." Ranger Stranger and Doc. Soleil had convinced her that Emily *really* was a help to them and that they actually *liked* having her around.

Emily didn't know why it was so hard to believe. It seemed her mom didn't like having her around, maybe she found it hard to think someone else might. When Emily thought about it too much her stomach hurt, her chest felt tight, and she missed her dad real bad, so she tried not to think about it.

"Your mom's depressed," the ranger explained, "because of your dad." He said depressed people have a hard time liking anyone, especially themselves. "Your mom loves you very much; she's just having a hard time showing it right now."

Emily didn't understand. "I'm sad about my dad, too."

"Sadness and depression are two different things, Emily. You and your mom will always be sad about losing your dad. Depression keeps your mom from enjoying her life. One of these days your mom will heal."

Emily felt better after talking with the ranger. She remembered Principal Sweaty-Pants getting so mad at her. *I'm sorry,* Emily wanted to say. *I don't mean to cause trouble or get in fights.* But every time she opened her mouth the words came out wrong. They spewed out of her like the pea soup that girl from *The Exorcist* puked. She couldn't help it. She guessed it was because she was depressed, like her mother. But it didn't happen so much now, so maybe she wasn't depressed any more.

Emily was restocking the shelves one morning at the ranger station when a family pulled up in a mini-van and came in. There was a mom and dad, a boy about Emily's age and a little girl who looked about seven years old.

While her parents went to the desk the little girl approached Emily and asked, "Do you work here?"

"Yes," Emily answered.

The girl eyed her suspiciously. "You don't look old enough to work."

"I just help out now and then," Emily admitted. "It's not like a real, grown-up job."

The girl's parents waited for the ranger to get off the phone and then asked, "Do you have any information on fishing?"

The forestry service had several pamphlets on fishing. Emily knew right where they were because she restocked them at least once a week. She went to the rack and grabbed the booklet entitled *Freshwater Fishing.*

"Here." She handed the booklet to the girl's older brother. He was a big kid—tall and chubby.

"Let me see it," the girl said, trying to snatch it out of the boy's hand.

"Don't." The boy pushed her away roughly.

"Mom!" the girl cried.

"Wait," Emily said. "I'll get you one too. You can have your own."

The girl smiled, grabbed the booklet from Emily's hands, and waved it under her brother's nose.

"We just got new fishing poles from the Big Pine Market," she said. "Mine's *The Little Mermaid* and his is stupid *Batman*."

"Where are you going fishing?" Emily asked.

"Just to the park across the street. We are going to fish off the dock."

Hanging around the ranger station Emily had heard plenty of talk about rainbow trout, brown trout, minnows and kokanee. "What are you trying to catch?" she asked.

"I just told you," the girl said with exasperation. "Fish!"

"And I bought some bacon at the store," the boy added. "Because the guy there said that I could catch crawdads with bacon. They're just like little lobsters. They scream when you throw them in a pot of boiling water."

"Eewww, that's so gross." The girl grimaced.

"All right, kids, you ready?" the dad asked.

"Yeah," they cried in unison. "Let's go fishing."

"Hey," the boy turned to Emily, "you want to come?"

Emily had never been fishing. "Sure," she said. "I'll meet you down at the lake when I'm done here."

The boy grinned, "I'm Ryan and the dodo brain," he pointed towards his sister, "is Amber. What's your name?"

"Emily."

"See you at the lake, Emily."

CHAPTER NINE

Emily rode her skateboard down the hill towards the beach carrying a bucket and some string she found in the back room of the ranger station. Lucky trotted happily by her side. She was a good dog. She never ran into the street or chased squirrels and she always came when Emily called her. Lucky seemed to understand that if she didn't behave she would be tethered to a leash, and she didn't like to be restrained. Not even when she was little and escaped the fenced yard of the people who owned her for one day. Emily never tied her up. Why would she? She loved Lucky and Lucky loved her. They were the same—free spirits—from the moment fate brought them together.

When Emily reached the bottom of the hill she could see Ryan and Amber at the end of the dock that jutted out into the blue, crystal clear waters of Emerald Lake. She jumped off her skateboard and walked down to the water's edge in search of a suitable rock. She was look-ing for a rock that fit easily into the palm of her hand. It needed to have rough, angular edges.

Lucky stayed further up on the beach preferring keep her delicate little feet dry. Emily didn't mind getting her feet wet as long as she wasn't wearing her good skateboarding shoes. The wet rocks were beautiful. Orangey-reds, rich golden browns, and shiny shades of black shimmered in the shallows. Some were striped, others speckled.

It amazed her how boring the rocks looked when they dried. Time after time she collected the most beautiful specimens and lined them up on the dock. By the time her mother came to see them, she'd yawn and shake her head. After drying in the warm summer sun, the rocks became plain old rocks again.

Wet rocks are like a big secret that most people don't get, like her mom and some classmates from school. Whenever the guys see her and Lucky one always yells, "That's the ugliest dog I've ever seen." Then another adds, "An ugly dog for an ugly girl." They laugh and laugh, like they've said something clever. But Lucky is a wet rock. If they knew her, like Emily did, they would know that Lucky was the most beautiful dog in the whole world.

The kids from the ranger station were sitting on the end of the dock baiting their fishing poles. A GI Joe tackle box sat open in the center of the dock surrounded by an assortment of fishing gear: single and tri-pronged hooks, lead tear-drop shaped sinkers, shiny metallic lures and lures made of soft rubber, red and white bubble floaters, delicate feathered flies, glass jars full of neon fish eggs and florescent orange cheese balls, needle-nosed pliers, scissors, a silver handled, green mesh fishing net, and an open pack of bacon.

Emily sat down at the edge of the mess and crossed her legs. Lucky lay down by her side. "What are you doing?" she asked.

"The fish don't like our fish eggs," Amber complained, "so I'm putting cheese balls on my hook." She had a huge hook on her line that was bigger than the mouths of any fish that Emily had seen off the dock—not that that was saying much.

"That's stupid," Ryan said. "They're probably not going to like those any better." Amber stuck her tongue out at him but he ignored her and continued speaking. "I'm going to put on one of these spinners." Ryan held up a shiny silver piece of metal that was twisted in half and had a hook on the end. "You see this? This spins around in the water when you reel it in. The fish think it's a minnow swimming and try to eat it. They really can't resist it. I'm going to catch a ton of fish with this baby."

"Wow, that's awesome," Emily said, and she meant it. "You guys have a lot of cool fishing stuff."

Emily pulled the string out of her bucket. "Can I have a piece of your bacon?" she asked.

"Sure."

She peeled loose a slice of bacon and cut a two-inch piece with the scissors.

Lucky leapt to her feet, tail wagging, and made a move towards the strip of raw meat.

"No, girl," Emily said sternly. "This is not for you."

Lucky whined, lay back down, and rested her head on her paws.

Emily tied the bacon to the end of her string. Then she measured up about a foot up from the bacon and tied the rock to it. She tugged on the string and was satisfied that the surface of the rock was rough enough to hold the string, which might slipped off a smooth rock.

"What are you doing?" Amber said, wiping her neon colored, cheese ball, slimed fingers on the front of her shirt.

"Going to catch some crawdads."

"With that?" Ryan hooted. "That's the dumbest thing I ever heard. You can't catch crawdads with string. You need a rig like this." He held up his Batman pole.

"The ranger showed me how to do this," Emily said.

"Naw," Ryan scoffed, "he probably just doesn't want you to play with hooks—he's afraid you'll hurt yourself."

"Yeah," Amber said, "he thinks you're a baby."

Emily ignored them. Lying on her belly on the warm wooden planks of the dock, she reached down with the bucket, and scooped up a few inches of water.

"Why did you do that?" Amber asked.

"Crawdads are like lobsters. You want to keep them alive until you eat them."

"Eeoww, that's disgusting. Are you really going to eat them?"

Emily had never actually eaten crawdads. Her mom had never been willing to cook them. But she wasn't about to admit it to these kids. Besides, this time she would cook and eat them all by herself. She would be twelve in two weeks and that was plenty old enough.

"Hush," Emily said, dropping the line into the water, "you'll scare them." She lay on her front and carefully guided her line between the cracks of two large rocks that were part of the docks foundation. She knew that's where the crawdads lived.

"I'm going to use some bacon too," the girl announced, "with my cheese balls. It'll be just like a bacon cheeseburger. The fish gotta love that!" She bent over her hook and added a strip of bacon to the already loaded barb.

Emily saw movement under the rock. Two little antennae came into view, then one pink claw and another. The crawdad marched up to the bacon, grasped it firmly in its claws, and began to pull it back to safety under the rock. Ever so slowly, Emily pulled up on her string. The crawdad, reluctant to give up the tasty meal, clung to the bacon as it rose in the water. "Get the net! Get the net!" she whispered urgently.

Ryan dropped his pole and ran to see what Emily was doing. Quickly he grabbed the net and used it to scoop the crawdad out of the water.

"Wow, we caught one. That's cool!" he shouted, as he stared at it through the dripping mesh.

"Quick, put it in the bucket," Emily said.

As Ryan reached into the net to grab the crawdad, it raised its claws like a ninja and clamped down on his index finger.

"Ouch!" he screamed, yanking his hand from the net. The crustacean was firmly attached to his finger and held on stubbornly as Ryan tried to shake it loose. Finally the crawdad flew into the sky and landed with a splash in the water. They watched it shoot backwards towards the rocks with a flash of its tail.

Ryan stuck his sore finger in his mouth, his eyes shining with excitement. "Hey, can I have a piece of string?"

"Yeah, me too?" Amber chimed in.

"I don't know." Emily's voice oozed sarcasm. "It's not fancy like your rig. You might not be able to catch anything with it."

The kids' faces fell.

"Oh, all right," Emily said. "Go get some rocks, and make sure they have rough edges."

A man wandered down the dock to see what they were doing. He showed them how to pick up "the little buggers" by the back of the neck so they couldn't pinch them with their claws.

The three kids were lined up on the dock like sardines. In fifteen minutes they caught nineteen crawdads. The bucket was filling up and each time they looked inside the crawdads all stood at attention like little soldiers, their weapons held high.

Lucky lay near their feet. Her eyes traveled back and forth between Emily and the piece of bacon that lay warming in the sun amongst the fishing gear. Emily didn't notice as Lucky scooted forward on her belly until she reached the bacon. She sniffed it and then licked it once and then looked back at Emily. She was busy fishing. Unable to resist, Lucky snatched the piece of bacon. She let out a yelp as something sharp cut her lip.

"Oh no!" Emily cried, when she realized what Lucky had done.

"Hey, your dog ate the bacon from my hook," Amber said.

"I'll get it," Ryan said, reaching for the Little Mermaid pole that had been discarded on the pier in favor of Emily's string.

"No!" Emily shouted, but it was too late.

Ryan yanked on the pole and the barbed hook punctured the skin of Lucky's top lip.

"You idiot!" Emily yelled. "Now we won't be able to pull it out."

"What are you going to do?" Amber asked fretfully.

"I've got to get her to Dr. Soleil. He'll know what to do." Emily picked up the pair of scissors and snipped the line. Gathering Lucky tenderly in her arms, she said, "I have to go."

"Hey, what about your crawdads?" Ryan asked.

"Throw them back," Emily called over her shoulder. "You'll never eat them, so you should let them live."

CHAPTER TEN

Running up the hill with Lucky in her arms was difficult. Emily's lungs hurt and a stitch stabbed her side. She was so winded when she reached the veterinary clinic that she could hardly speak.

Missy was at the front desk when Emily exploded through the door. One look at her and Missy dropped what she was doing and ran to help.

"What happened?" she cried.

Emily's face was flushed, her chest heaving. "She has...a hook...stuck...in her lip."

"Sure enough," Missy said, looking closely at Lucky's mouth. "Let me get Karen."

Karen waddled in and examined Lucky. "No big deal...happens around here a lot. You're just in time. We were closing up for lunch. Taking the dog from Emily she said, "Follow me." Her belly was so big it looked like Lucky was resting on a beanbag chair. She set Lucky on the examining table of the first treatment room and went to get Dr. Soleil.

The vet paused in the doorway, shaking his head at the sight of the unkempt girl with her tear stained face and her equally disheveled mutt. Emily's passion for life and her capacity for love, in spite of what appeared to be a life marred by sadness, neglect and a certain amount of dirt, astonished him. *Thank God she has that dog.*

He entered the room and said, "Let's take a look." He looked at Lucky's lip and then reached into a drawer and pulled out a pair of wire snips.

"What are you going to do?" Emily asked fearfully.

"I can't back the hook out, it pierced the skin. The barb would tear up her lip if I tried to pull it back out. So, I am going to cut the barb off the hook using these wire snips and then I'll be able to back the hook out. You're going to have to hold Lucky steady for me. Do you think you can do that, Emily?"

She nodded and then wrapped her arms around the dog and held her tight.

In less than a second he was done. He dabbed antibiotic ointment on Lucky's swollen lip. She wagged her tail and looked as good as new.

The vet dropped the wire snips into a tray of green liquid. "I was just going to make a peanut butter sandwich for lunch and go sit outside to enjoy the nice day. Do you want to join me?" he asked.

"Sure," Emily said. "I'm starving!"

She followed him to the break room. He handed her a loaf of bread, the peanut butter, jelly, and a knife. She made sandwiches while he gathered plates, napkins, soft drinks, seedless grapes and cookies. They piled everything onto a tray and carried it out back to a picnic table. The day was warm and the air smelled of pine. Every now and then a soft breeze rustled the tops of the trees making them sway like hula girls.

Emily took a bite of her sandwich, looked Dr. Soleil in the eye and asked, "So how many days am I going to have to work to pay for this visit?"

He was pleased to see her addressing the situation rather than ignoring it, or worse, whining like a brat. It showed she took her responsibility for the dog seriously and felt the need to pay her debts. Concerned that she was running around unsupervised all summer, he considered his answer carefully. He wanted to tell her she needed to work the rest of the summer, just so he could keep an eye on her. On the other hand, he wanted to encourage her developing sense of responsibility and he wasn't going to do that by over-charging her.

"Humm." He licked peanut butter from his fingers as he thought about the best thing to do. "This visit was worth about...uh...5 hours of pay. I think you've got a little time still on the books from taking care of the boarders—you're doing a great job with them by the way, so keep it up. Check with Missy on your hours and ask her if she needs help with anything."

"Okay." Emily took another bite of her sandwich. She was glad to have another legitimate reason to work at the clinic. She loved it but her mother was still griping, convinced Emily was making a nuisance of herself. Emily worried that one-day her mother would forbid her from visiting the ranger station or the clinic altogether.

Karen waddled out the rear door and down the steps to the picnic table. "Emily, did you want this?" She held up a little specimen jar with the pieces of the hook inside. "Missy and I are going to the store to pick up a few groceries and we'll have our lunch there. See you soon."

Emily looked at the bits of curved and sharpened metal in the plastic jar. She remembered the pain in her stomach when she heard Lucky yelp and realized what happened.

"Did you know?" she said turning the specimen bottle around in her hands, "Czar Peter the Great cut off the head of one of his girlfriend's boyfriend, put it in a jar of alcohol, and stuck it on the table by her bed."

Dr. Soleil looked at her in astonishment.

"Oh, I'm sorry." Emily looked distressed. "Mom gets mad at me when I talk about stuff like that, especially while we're eating."

Dr. Soleil started laughing. "It's okay, Emily. You've got to tell me how you know all these strange things."

She took another bite of her sandwich and stared off in the distance for so long that he wondered if he'd lost her.

"My dad..." she finally said, "my dad taught European history at the university. His specialty was European royalty. He loved to tell his students all this crazy stuff about the royalty because A), it got their attention and B), it made them seem less glamorous and more like regular people."

"You were close to your dad?"

"Yeah," she nodded.

"What happened?"

"Princess Diana died."

"Huh?"

"We went to England last summer to tour British castles and battle fields and stuff, and so I could see where Emily Bronte lived and where Mary, Queen of Scots, lived and so Dad could do some research. We had just returned to London from touring Scotland...we were getting packed to go home the next day...school was starting in a week...we heard the news...Princess Diana was...dead...car accident."

"I don't understand," Dr. Soleil said gently.

"We...were upset. Everyone in London was upset. Dad said that Princess Diana was 'the queen of hearts'. Mom said Prince Charles should have died instead because he'd been such a jerk. My dad's name was Charles too... you know?"

Dr. Soleil nodded, although he hadn't known.

"Dad always said that Diana was the best thing to happen to British royalty in centuries. He was crazy about her. Used to joke that the reason he married my mom was that Princess Diana was taken. He married 'the next best Diana'. He was joking." Emily glanced at Dr. Soleil to make sure he understood.

He nodded.

"Anyway," she continued, "we bought a bouquet of flowers for her and left it outside the fence at Buckingham palace. There were lots and lots of flowers and cards and teddy bears and all sorts of stuff. We couldn't believe it. It was incredible.

"My dad was so upset that day. He said his stomach hurt way up high." Emily patted her belly just below her breastbone. "Mom said it wasn't his stomach—it was his heart. She said he had a broken heart...you know...because of Diana being the queen of hearts. But my dad's pain didn't go away. When we got home Mom took him to the hospital where she worked. She's a nurse, you know?"

Dr. Soleil nodded. No, he hadn't known that either.

"The doctor from Mom's hospital said Dad had pancreatic cancer and he only had a few months to live." Emily wasn't hungry any more. She leaned down and gave the last of her sandwich to Lucky who was curled up by her feet. Lucky took the sandwich and ate it like her lip didn't hurt one bit.

"I'm sorry, Emily," Dr. Soleil said.

Emily nodded and looked off in the distance at the swaying treetops. "Dad went into the hospital the day after Thanksgiving...Mom was his nurse. I went to school...stayed with my friend, Amy...until Mom got home for dinner. We went to see him every night during visiting hours.

"They said Dad wouldn't make it until Christmas, but he did. We took all the presents in Christmas morning...there weren't many. Mom had forgotten to buy any—I already knew about Santa so it was okay—but other people sent stuff and my grandma brought gifts for everybody. Don't know if Dad even knew we were there. He wasn't talking any more...not even opening his eyes. When we left that day Mom said it was time to say 'goodbye' forever. I held his hand for a long time...begged him to get better, until Mom said it was time to go."

"Hi." The Ranger came around the corner and interrupted their conversation. "Some kids came by the station and dropped off Emily's skateboard and my bucket. They told me what happened to Lucky. Is she okay?"

Emily looked blankly at the Ranger. Her eyes were haunted and seemed to look right through him. She blinked a few times, pulled herself back into the present, and then grinned. Pointing under the table, she said, "Look for yourself."

Hearing her name, Lucky jumped up and greeted the Ranger warmly. He picked her up and let her lick his neck and face before setting her back down.

"Things look pretty serious around here. What's up?" he asked.

"Emily was just telling me about when her dad died earlier this year. Did you know that Emily's mom is a nurse?"

"You're kidding. I didn't know that. Why is she working at the store, Emily?"

"She tried to go back after Dad died but she couldn't. She loved being a nurse but she couldn't deal with sick people anymore—they made her cry—and she totally freaked if someone died. So the hospital made her take time off until she gets better. She stayed home, sat around in her bathrobe all day crying, and then she started drinking.

"Grandma was coming by a lot. One day Grandma said she wanted to take me home to live with her. Mom went ballistic and they got into a big fight. Mom threw Grandma out of the house and told her never to come back. I haven't seen her since." Emily flicked crumbs off the table with her fingernail. "I miss her," she said. "And then we came here. Mom's friend from the hospital thought it might help to get away for a while. She arranged for us to rent the cabin for a year from her aunt. Voila! Here we are."

"Is it helping?" the ranger asked.

"I don't know." Emily's eyes darkened. "I think since Dad died, Mom... she...uh...doesn't care about anything anymore—not even me." A tear leaked from the corner of her eye and slid down her cheek.

Dr. Soleil came around the table and lifted her into his arms and held her as she struggled to maintain her composure. For the first time in a very long time, Emily allowed herself to be comforted.

CHAPTER ELEVEN

"*H*ush everybody, here she comes!"

Giggles and whispers erupted from inside the clinic as people gathered around the windows vying for the first glimpse of Emily and Lucky walking up the street.

"How did you get her to come?" the Ranger asked.

"I told her we had a litter of puppies staying over the weekend and asked her to come by to feed them, since we close early on Saturdays."

"That'll do it. She loves puppies."

"Hey, did anyone think to call her mom?" Dr. Soleil asked.

"No, it never occurred to me." Missy shrugged apologetically.

"We should have," Karen added.

"It's not too late. Quick, Missy, give Diana a call before Emily walks in. She really should be here, too."

Emily walked up to the front door of the clinic. "That's strange," she said to Lucky as she reached for the door handle. "I wonder why the lights are off inside. Dr. Soleil usually leaves a light on after he closes."

Lucky looked at her and wagged her fluffy tail.

"Surprise!"

Emily jumped and let out a yelp.

"Happy Birthday, Emily."

Emily couldn't believe it. She'd never in her life had a surprise party. She stood in the doorway, hands crossed over her racing heart, grinning broadly.

Karen lumbered up to her carrying a huge balloon bouquet. She had one arm wrapped around her enormous belly and a two-year-old clinging to her leg. She gave Emily a quick hug and then hobbled back to stand by her husband, Sal. He was a loud, cheerful guy whom Emily had met once before and liked instantly.

Missy ran up, hugged her and introduced her to her husband, Warren. He was tall and balding, with intense eyes and a beak nose. He smiled stiffly and offered a weak handshake.

Ranger Stranger was there with the whole Stranger family, including his son Tyler. Tyler was hot. He was also way older than Emily, at least 16, and probably had only come for the food.

"Look who I found," the ranger said. He stepped aside to reveal the fishing kids, Ryan and Amber. They smiled and waved shyly.

"I can't believe it," Emily said happily.

"Come on, everyone, dinner is served. There's pizza and cold drinks out back." The vet ushered the crowd towards the door.

Emily followed the group and was amazed to find even more balloons tied to every surface; chairs, tree limbs and deck rails. The bathtub was filled with brightly colored packages.

"Wow, all this is for me?"

"Of course, sweetie," Missy said, "it's your birthday tomorrow. You didn't think we'd let that slip by without noticing, did you?"

Emily blinked back unexpected tears and smiled.

"Go get some pizza, honey, before it gets cold."

Emily picked a huge slice of pepperoni pizza and took a bite from it. She could feel warm oil drip down her chin, and wiped it with her sleeve. Missy frowned at her from across the table and handed her a napkin. She grinned, then went over to say "Hi" to Ryan and Amber.

"I thought you went home," Emily said.

"Yeah, well our parents are thinking of buying a cabin here so we'll be coming back on the weekends to look at property."

"That would be cool to have you guys around."

"It would just be for summers," Amber said, "while we're out of school. My dad works in the city."

"My dad says we're going to get a speed boat," Ryan added, "so we can take you water skiing."

"Wow," Emily said. "That would be awesome."

Emily went to the ice-filled cooler for a soft drink and came face to face with the ranger's son, Tyler. Her heart danced.

"It's your birthday, huh?" he said.

Emily cocked an eyebrow.

"Okay," he laughed. "I guess that was kinda lame. Let me try again. I've seen you skating around town. Can you do any tricks on that board?"

"I used to be able to do some," she said, "just some ollies and stuff. We used to have a skate park near our old house. Now I mostly use it to get places."

"There's a skate park over in Bear Creek. Next time my buddies and I go maybe you can come along."

"Really! That would be so cool. Thanks!" Emily blushed. She was acutely aware of pizza sauce on her upper lip. She licked it with the tip of her tongue and looked to see if Tyler had noticed.

A car roared up the street and screeched to a stop. Emily's mother stepped unsteadily from the car and held up a large bottle of wine. "Okay, I'm here and I brought refreshments." She walked up to the table, set the bottle down and looked around. "Wow, this is quite a shindig, Emily. Why don't you introduce me to your friends."

"Okay, Mom." Emily felt a sinking feeling in the pit of her stomach as she took her mother's hand. She walked her mother around the yard taking the time to introduce her to everyone. As she did she noticed flickers of judgment cross their faces and she felt a mixture of shame and embarrassment as well as a desire to protect her mother.

"How on earth did you make all these friends without me knowing?" Diana asked, smiling brightly—too brightly.

"You've been busy, Mom, that's all," Emily said. "Here, take a seat. I'll get you some pizza."

"No honey, I'm not hungry. I just want a little glass of wine."

Dr. Soleil crept up behind them and snapped their picture with his instamatic camera. "Allow me," he said, offering Emily's mother a molded plastic chair with a pair of helium balloons tied to the back. "Have a seat. Keep the chair from floating off." He winked, then returned a moment later with a plastic glass, half-filled, which he handed to Diana.

She eyed it with irritation.

"I'm glad you could come," he said. "Means a lot to Emily."

"It does?" Sarcasm oozed from Diana Locke's lips. "You could have fooled me. She didn't even bother to invite me. I should ground her for being so sneaky."

"Mom!" Emily's stomach twisted in that painfully familiar way. "It was a surprise party. I didn't know about it either."

"It's my fault, Mrs. Locke. Please, forgive me for not calling you earlier. This was just a casual, last minute idea. It came together quickly and we truly didn't mean to overlook you. We just wanted Emily to have a nice birthday."

"She's my daughter. You don't think I'd have seen to that? I had big plans for her birthday tomorrow. I was going to take her...uh...to...uh...."

"Mrs. Locke. I truly meant no offense. Please forgive me."

Diana, looking faintly mollified, took a sip from her glass.

The back door opened and Missy came out carrying a cake. It was decorated with brightly colored balloons made from frosting and said *Happy Birthday Emily* on it in blue. Twelve candles burned brightly across the top.

Karen hastily moved the empty pizza boxes off the picnic table to make room.

"Okay, Emily," Missy set the cake down on the table in front of her. "Come over here and make a wish."

Emily closed her eyes and thought real hard. *I wish...I wish that I would always feel this lucky.* Then she bent down and blew out every single candle to the applause and cheers of everyone.

"Who wants cake?" Missy started slicing wedges. "Emily, do you want the piece with the balloons or the piece with your name on it? Or both?"

"The balloons have more frosting—I want them."

"I'll bring you your piece, Emily. Sit down on the steps over there. You have presents to open."

Emily sat on the top step, which leads from the rear deck to the grassy yard below. Ryan and Amber nominated themselves gift-getters and brought her packages from the tub.

"Here, open ours first," Amber said. She handed Emily two packages. One was long and thin and the other rectangular, about the size of a shoebox. They were both wrapped in matching pink paper. Emily took the first package and laughed. "Gee, I wonder what this is?"

"A fishing pole," Amber announced, unable to restrain herself. "The Little Mermaid. I picked it out myself. Now you have a pole just like mine."

"Thanks!" Emily tore off the paper and admired her new pole. "Maybe we can go fishing tomorrow."

"Quick! Open the next one. Guess what it is." Amber was bouncing with excitement, and Ryan had moved in closely beside her.

Emily opened the second package and found a matching Little Mermaid tackle box filled with the same cool stuff that they had in theirs.

"Wow, this is great." Before Emily could finish looking at her new gear, Amber snatched it from her and handed her another package.

It was thin, rectangular—felt like a book—and wrapped in a sheet from the Sunday comics. She turned it over and looked for a tag.

Dr. Soleil kneeled in front of her and took a close-up shot with his camera. "That's from me," he said. "Open it."

Inside she found a small photo album—a brag book—with *Surprise!* stamped across the front.

"You can put the pictures from this party in it." Dr. Soleil held up the camera. "So you can always remember it. I'll have them developed tomorrow."

"Thanks," she said. Amber snatched it from her hands and replaced it with a new gift.

Emily looked at the tag and saw that it was from the ranger and his family. She looked up and saw them smiling at her. It was a big, square box—big enough for a basketball. She shook it. Nope, not a basketball—too soft. She tore off the paper, opened the box and peered inside. A Smokey the Bear stuffed animal and a Smokey the Bear tee shirt. I love them," she said pulling them from the box. The ranger had them for sale at the station. She'd always wanted them but never thought she'd get them.

She crossed the yard to thank the Ranger and his wife. Tyler snatched the bear from her arms and tossed it to Ryan who threw it back, shouting, "Keep Away!" Emily tried to intercept her bear, while Lucky raced back and forth between the two boys barking wildly. Amber squealed with delight, clapping her hands and jumping up and down on her tippy-toes.

Karen's two-year-old toddled up to the empty box and carried it away in his chubby hands. He crossed the yard, set it down and started filling it with pinecones. His dad followed after him carrying a large slice of cake in hand. Dr. Soleil helped himself to a second piece of cake and Emily's mom refilled her glass.

Things finally settled down and Emily resumed opening gifts. Amber handed her another huge box—this one even bigger than the last. What could it be, Emily wondered. She shook it. It sounded much like the last one.

"This is from all of us at the Clinic," Dr. Soleil said. "Missy and Karen did the shopping, so if you have any problems with any of it, talk to them."

Emily tore off the brightly colored paper and lifted the lid off the box. She looked inside and saw a couple of tissue wrapped layers. She reached into the box and pulled the top layer from the tissue. A pair of denim shorts and a red tank top with the words, *Life's a Beach*, splashed across the front in blue and yellow. She held the shirt up to herself and smiled as Dr. Soleil snuck in for another picture. She reached back into the box. This time she pulled out a pale blue, velveteen, sweat suit with a zippered jacket and low cut pants with a little jeweled heart on the thigh.

"I love it." She smiled brightly. Looking back in the box, she said, "Wow. There's more?"

"Let me see, honey." Diana walked over and sat down next to Emily on the step. She looked at each outfit as Emily reached back into the box. This time she pulled out a pair of low-waisted cargo pants and soft cotton, floral print, peasants blouse." The blouse was beautiful. She couldn't wait to try them on.

"Look Mom, can you believe it? Don't you love it?"

"What's with all the clothes?" Diana turned on Emily and hissed, "Look at you. You look like some ragamuffin orphan. No wonder everyone thinks they have to buy you clothes."

"No, Mom. Not now. Please." Emily begged.

"Why don't you dress decently instead of making me look like a bad mother?"

"Mom!" Emily looked around to see if anyone was listening.

"Answer me, young lady."

"I don't have much that fits me any more, Mom. I've been trying to tell you."

Diana's eyes flashed. "Give this back," she gathered the clothes in her arms and threw them back in the box. "You're not a charity case."

"No, mom! Stop! Please stop it and go home!"

"I am going home and you're going with me."

"No," Emily stood up and ran down the steps.

"Emily Mary Locke, come back here. Right now!" Diana called after her.

"Take a hike!" Emily turned and yelled, and then she ran off into the woods as fast as her legs would carry her. She ran away from her crazy mother. She ran away from the bewildered eyes and the slack jaws of her guests. She ran away from the cute boy, Tyler, who looked at her like she was a child. She ran and ran and Lucky ran with her.

Finally she reached a secluded spot in the woods with a broad stump cut at sitting height. She pulled Lucky into her arms and held her close. Sitting cross-legged on the stump, she started to weep. "Why is Mom crazy," she sniffed. "Why did she have to ruin my birthday?"

A twig snapped in the wooded shadows behind her and Emily hastily wiped her eyes and turned.

"Take a hike?" Dr. Soleil stepped into the clearing and planted himself in front of her with his hands on his hips. "That's pretty disrespectful, don't you think?"

"She deserved it," Emily said crossly.

"You know what they say about two wrongs, Emily...."

"I know, I know," she admitted. "Besides it wasn't really wrong. I mean she could stand to take a good hike. It would be relaxing for her, and good exercise."

"What's next? Go jump in the lake?"

"Well, she does like to swim," Emily ventured.

"Emily!" He waited.

"Okay. I'm sorry. I'll tell her I'm sorry."

Dr. Soleil smiled. "Atta girl."

Emily hugged Lucky to her and took a deep breath. "What happened back there? Is everything all right?"

Everything's fine. Your mom apologized and Ranger Wade offered to drive her home. Emily, your mom's going through a difficult time. Everyone understands."

"She didn't used to be like this," Emily said. "I just want my old mom back."

"Give her time." Dr. Soleil reached out his hand to her. "Come on, Emily, I'll walk you home. Your mom's worried about you."

"What about my...umm..."

"Your presents? You're mom took them home with her."

"Okay," Emily sighed and took his hand. They walked in silence. The interwoven branches blocked much of the light from the sprinkling of stars that had started to appear overhead. They chose each step carefully, stepping over fallen branches and pinecones, as they followed a short cut through the woods towards Emily's house. When they finally reached her yard, Emily stopped and turned to him. "Thank you, Dr. Soleil, for everything. That was a wonderful party." She gave him a quick hug and ran to her front door.

CHAPTER TWELVE

Emily nudged open the cabin door just enough to poke her head in. She was a little leery about seeing her mom after the fiasco at the party, even though Dr. Soleil assured her everything was okay. She had so many conflicting emotions soaring through her, colliding and exploding, like a scene from *Star Wars*. She needed some time to sort things through.

The house seemed dark and quiet—unusually so. Dusk had settled like chocolate syrup on the bottom of a glass. Her mom hadn't bothered to turn on a light. Closing the door behind her, Emily tiptoed into the room.

"Mom?" she called, her voice barely above a whisper. The TV stood mute in the corner next to the fireplace. *Usually Mom falls asleep on the couch during a show and doesn't turn it off until she goes to bed. But maybe....* Emily peeked over the couch and found it empty. Concern pricked her spine. "Mom?" She called a little louder this time with bravado in her voice that she didn't feel. "I'm home."

Suddenly she heard a sound coming from the rear of the cabin where their bedrooms were located. The hair on her scalp and neck rose with goose bumps. She crept to the doorway and peered down the hall. A light haloed the edges of her bedroom door. *It's in my room.* Her heart skipped a beat. Holding her breath, she tiptoed silently towards the doorway. Lucky seemed to understand and padded softly behind her without the usual clicking of her nails against the hardwood floors.

When she reached her room she held an eye to the narrow crack of light where the door stood slightly ajar. She could see her mother sitting cross-legged on the floor in front of her dresser drawers. The bottom drawer was open. The one where Emily put all the clothes that no longer fit her. The one that was so jammed full it barely closed anymore. One by one her mother pulled a shirt or a pair of pants from the drawer and held it up in front of her. "This looks like it fits," she muttered, holding up a pair of jeans.

"It doesn't, Mom." Emily pushed open the door and leaned against the doorjamb. She noticed piles of clothes scattered about her bedroom floor. Lucky sniffed a few of them then choose the largest one to lie down on. She rolled onto her back and wriggled contentedly. Emily was relieved to see her new birthday gifts stacked neatly on her bed.

Diana looked at her daughter, her eyes filled with anguish. "I don't believe you," she said angrily. "Try them on."

Emily stripped off her shorts, took the jeans from her mother and stepped into them. She pulled them up as high as her thighs and then started to struggle. "Maybe if I lie down," she muttered, thinking of the models she'd seen on TV who fought to fit into skin-tight jeans."

"No, never mind. Take them off. Try this top on."

Emily pulled off her tee shirt and then stuck her arms in the pink My Little Pony shirt. A favorite, it had been difficult to surrender to the bottom drawer. Struggling, she finally pulled the shirt over her head and down over her torso. It was skintight and Emily felt short of breath wearing it.

"Oh." Diana stared at the shirt that clung to Emily's chest, revealing every curve and bump. "Take it off," she cried.

Emily struggled to peel the shirt back over her head.

"Take it off!"

"I'm trying!"

"How did this happen?"

Emily didn't answer. She could tell her mother was no longer talking to her. She was talking to herself as if Emily wasn't in the room. It made her feel uneasy when her mom did that. She usually did it when she was really unhappy.

"How could this happen?" Her mother's focus sharpened but her tone softened. "You've grown up right in front of my eyes and I never noticed." She cupped her head with both hands and shook it gently. "What's wrong with me? My own daughter—how could I have missed it?"

"It's okay, Mom," Emily said.

"No, it's not okay, Emily. I've been a terrible mother lately." Tears filled her eyes. "I'm so sorry."

"Mom...." Emily felt helpless.

"I am, Emily. I've been half crazy since your dad died. I miss him so much. I've been so caught up in my own loss that I'm neglecting you—my precious little girl." Diana sniffed and wiped her nose on her sleeve. "I love you. You're everything to me. I'm so sorry, Emily," she said miserably, wiping the trail of mascara that ran down her cheek with the back of her hand. She was left with black eyes and a bruise-like smudge across one cheek, like she'd boxed eight rounds. "Can you ever forgive me?"

Emily fought back tears, swallowed hard and nodded.

"Come here, baby." Diana beckoned her with open arms.

Emily crawled into her mother's lap. The emotion she'd held back for so long flooded through her. She clung to her mother and for the first time since her father died, they cried together.

Diana rocked Emily in her arms. "From now on things are going to be different, baby. I promise," she said.

CHAPTER THIRTEEN

Emily kept her head down and her eyes glued to the bowl as she shoveled another spoonful of granola into her mouth. Her mother was having one of her early morning freak-outs and Emily knew from experience that this was one of those times when patience was a virtue.

"I'm working all day today and after work I'm going to my group-grief."

Emily nodded. This was the fifth time her mother had repeated this. After Emily's birthday, her mother had signed up for therapy. Twice a month she saw her counselor and each week she met with her grief support group for, uh... group support for her grief. She was doing better which was good, except for when it wasn't. The less depressed her mother was the less she drank, and the less she drank the more attention she paid to Emily—in other words, the more she stuck her nose into Emily's business. Having gotten used to coming and going pretty much as she chose, Emily was experiencing some difficulty readjusting to a motherly type of mother. Be careful what you wish for, they always say. It's like wishing to be queen, Emily figured, and marrying King Henry VIII, who had some of his many wives beheaded. Only this time it felt like her head was on the platter.

"Can you just come home after work? Maybe we can go to a movie or something?" Emily said.

"I'm sorry, sweetheart. You know I can't miss my session. They say it's very important to keep coming on a regular basis. It's early in my recovery. I need the group. They really understand what I'm going through."

"What about what I'm going through?"

"Oh, Emily, please! I know this is tough on you too, but can you just give me a break?"

Emily scowled. "Go to your dumb group—your Die and Cry buddies."

Diana stopped what she was doing and looked Emily in the eye. "Don't make fun, Emily. I don't know what I would do without all these wonderful people. I felt so isolated after your dad died—so disconnected. These people understand my pain. Every one of them has suffered horrible...horrible losses. We're helping pull each other out of that deep, dark, pit. I can't do it alone."

Emily groaned and looked down at her cereal bowl.

"Tomorrow's my day off. We'll have all day together."

"Can we go hiking?" Emily asked. "These people at the ranger station told me about a great day-hike to Lake Lupine. We can have a picnic."

"Are you kidding?" Diana shook her head. "I wish I could, but I've got to do laundry tomorrow, and clean the house. And I need to hunker down and pay that stack of bills that has been growing all month. Besides, the last thing I want to do after spending all week on my feet at work is to do it again on my day off. Maybe we can rent a video or something. That'll be fun."

Emily rolled her eyes. "Yeah, sure. I can hardly wait."

Diana's eyes blazed. "You know, young lady, you can cut the attitude any time now. I'm sick to death of your complaining."

"Apparently not," Emily said, "you appear very much alive to me."

"Emily!"

"You just wish you were 'sick to death'. Then you'd have something else to complain about to your friends. After all, misery loves company."

"Emily Mary Locke, I'm warning you."

"Just go already, you're going to be late. Leave me alone."

Diana sucked in a deep breath. "Okay, then. You know the rules. Do you think you'll be going to the ranger station or the vet's?"

"Yeah, maybe," Emily lied. She knew precisely what she was doing today and it didn't involve either of those places.

"Good. You need supervised activities. There's peanut butter and jelly for lunch, and I bought a frozen pizza for you to have for dinner."

"Okay, Mom."

"Remember to set the timer."

"I will, Mom."

"And don't forget to turn off the oven when you're done. And clean up your darn mess."

"Mom, you're going to be late."

Diana glanced at her watch and her eyes widened. "Oh no, I better fly. Be good. I'll see you when I get home."

"Yeah, sure."

"Oh, and Emily?"

"Yes, Mom?"

"Stay off that skateboard." Diana called over her shoulder as she raced out the door. "I don't want you getting hurt while I'm gone."

"Heaven forbid," Emily muttered as the door closed behind her mother. "That might mess up your busy schedule. Although you might get extra points with your group—5 points for scraped knees, 50 for a broken bone, and you hit the jackpot if I manage to kill myself."

Lucky responded by wagging her tail and barking sharply.

Emily listened carefully for the sound of tires screeching out of the driveway and the high-pitched whine of the engine as her mother gunned it in an effort to make up for lost time. She had memorized this sound by heart. Her mother was perpetually late and she always tried to make up the time by driving like Dale Earnhart or Richard Petty. Emily had no doubt that her mother could hold her own in the Indy 500—shoot, she'd probably win by a mile.

Once she was satisfied she was alone, Emily went to her room to gather her things. She brought out her backpack, a thick hard-cover book, a recreational map of the area, her wildlife and plant field guide, a tube of cherry Chapstick and a couple of Band-aids and lined them up on the kitchen table. Turning to the counter, she pulled out a loaf of bread and made herself a sandwich and stuck it in a baggie. Then she grabbed a chocolate chip granola bar from the cupboard and a big, juicy, navel orange from a bowl on the kitchen counter. She cut off the top of the orange with a knife and scored the sides—like her mother always did—to make it easier to peel later. She grabbed a bottle of water from the refrigerator, and then, on second thought, grabbed two more.

The Ranger had been talking about this thing, giardia, an amoeba they were finding in the water. It could get inside you and make you sick if you drank from the streams or lake while you were hiking in the wilderness. He said people needed to bring their own water on hikes.

Emily looked at the food she'd assembled and frowned. She was forgetting something. Suddenly she remembered. She smacked herself in the head with the palm of her hand. Grabbing another baggie, she filled it with dog biscuits. Now she was ready.

She was stashing the gear in her backpack when she was startled by the sound of someone climbing the front steps. *Oh, no. Mom forgot something!* Her heart thumped so hard that it felt like it might leap out of her chest and flop around on the floor like a fish out of water.

Tap, tap, tap. Someone knocked lightly.

Emily let out a sigh of relief. *Mom wouldn't knock so it can't be her.* She reached up on her tiptoes and leaned her eye against the peephole. At first she didn't see anyone at all, then she looked down.

Amber was just lifting her fist to knock again when Emily opened the door. "Hi, Amber. When did you get here?"

"We drove up last night."

"What are you doing?"

"I don't know. My mom told me that I was driving her crazy and to go outside and play, so I thought I'd come here. What are you doing?" Amber's eyes settled on the backpack and then the lunch. "Hey, are you going somewhere? Can I come?"

Emily regarded the girl doubtfully. "How far can you walk?"

"I can walk a long, long way. I walked all the way from our cabin to here."

"That's only a couple of blocks. Can you walk a couple of miles?"

"Well, I don't know. I can if you can," Amber challenged. "But we better hurry because my Mom said I have to be back in half an hour to go shopping."

"Well, forget it then, you can't come."

"Can I go with you some other time?" Amber asked as she sat down at the table and picked up the granola bar.

"Sure, Amber, some other time. Put that back. It's my lunch."

Amber dropped the granola bar. "Hey, is this that book you were reading last week?" She picked up the heavy book. "What is it?"

"It's called *Harry Potter and the Philosopher's Stone.*"

"Is it good?"

"It's really good."

"It looks hard." She meant long. "Does it have any pictures?"

"I promise you'd like it. You should read it sometime. Except you can't."

"Could too. I'm a good reader. I'm in the sparrow reading group in my class at school."

"No, you can't because you can't buy it here."

"What? You mean at the store? Why not?"

"My dad bought this for me on my birthday last summer in England when we were there. It's written by a British lady."

"Why don't they have it here?"

"I think they will soon, but the American version is called Harry Potter and the Sorcerer's Stone. Ask the bookstore."

"What's it about?"

"It's about a boy, both of his parents are dead, and people are really mean to him and they don't understand him at all. But he's a wizard and he uses magic to get back at all the horrible people. He does all kinds of crazy things to them."

"I wish I could do magic. I'd turn Ryan into a giant toad."

Emily laughed. "And I'd turn Principal Sweaty-pants into a fly so Ryan could eat her for lunch."

"Eeouw." Amber's eyes twinkled. "Yeah, that's perfect. Or, no! Maybe I'd turn Ryan into an ant and then I could step on him and squish him. Or maybe a monkey so everyone would laugh at him."

"I get it!"

"What's a Slitheren?" Amber said, pointing at a word on a page in the open book.

"Huh?"

"You always say, 'Son of a Slithern', and it's in this book."

"You're just going to have to read it to find out. By the way, you better get going if you need to be home in a half-hour."

"Oh, yeah. What time is it?" Amber jumped up and ran for the door. "Bye. See you later. Maybe I can come back after we're done shopping."

"You do that," Emily said closing the door behind her. "But, poof, like magic, I'll be gone."

CHAPTER FOURTEEN

Emily steered her bike carefully onto the rough, unpaved surface of the wilderness trailhead parking lot. She hopped off, leaned it against a towering cedar and wiped her brow with the sleeve of her sweatshirt. Then she lifted Lucky from the basket mounted to her handlebars and set her down. "Whew, girl, that was the longest ride ever." Lucky wagged her tail, barked twice, and then sniffed the base of the tree trunk. Emily could tell that Lucky loved riding up front in the basket, with the wind in her face and snout in the air, barking at passing motorists. *She loves it because she doesn't have to do the work.* She pulled a water bottle from her backpack and took a long swig. Then she kneeled down and poured water into her cupped hand, which Lucky gratefully lapped.

After stowing her water and locking her bike to the trunk of the tree with a coiled cable that barely stretched around the cedar's ancient girth, she prepared to hit the trail. She noticed a walking stick that someone had left leaning against the trail head sign for another hiker to use. She picked it up to see how it felt. It was really just a downed branch about an inch in diameter and four feet long, but it was straight and solid. Just holding it made Emily feel like an official hiker.

Emily started down the dusty trail, across a field of aspen towards the base of the mountain that rose dauntingly before her. "Come on, Lucky," she called, each time the dog veered off the path to chase a squirrel. The morning light reflected off leaves that whispered with the cool breeze, throwing a kaleidoscope of light and color along the path. In the distance, she could hear the faint rumble of a stream crashing over rocks and splashing into pools.

Soon Emily and Lucky left the wooded glen and began to climb. The path narrowed as it zigzagged up the mountain. Their steps became more difficult as they navigated the large rocks and bare tree roots that turned the trail into an obstacle course.

The roar of the water grew until it drowned out the other woodland sounds. They were getting close. Rounding a corner they found a bridge of rough-hewn logs spanning a narrow gorge where water gushed through and spilled on the rocks below, exploding in a thundering cloud of mist. They raced to the bridge and stood on it, facing the raging water. The force of the water pushed against them, they had to lean into it to keep their footing. A fine icy spray beaded their eyelashes and dripped down their noses. Emily shivered and Lucky shook herself vigorously.

A pair of backpackers, tanned and lean, squeezed past them on the bridge. Their packs bulged with gear, yet their steps were light and quick as though the packs were filled with helium. Emily watched them with a mixture of fascination and longing. She dreamed of the day when she was old enough to go backpacking in the woods for days at a time if she felt like it. She couldn't wait to be grown-up. Then she could do whatever she wanted, whenever she wanted, and nobody could tell her what to do. When she grew up, she'd leave so fast her mother's head would spin like a top, and she would never, ever, EVER come back.

"Come on, Lucky, we better get going if we're going to make it to Lake Lupine by lunch time."

The exertion of climbing the dusty trail, which had again turned to switchbacks, quickly warmed them. Emily was beginning to groan with each thigh-burning step. And Lucky, who earlier had chased every squirrel she saw, settled into the lead, expending no more energy than necessary to follow the trail. Every so often she'd look back to make sure Emily was still behind her, her little pink tongue hanging from the side of her mouth.

The sun was high in the cloudless sky by the time they reached a clearing near the top of the mountain where the trail split. Wooden signs, pointing in opposite directions, labeled the trails and distances. Emily sat on a rock to catch her breath. Lucky flopped down in the center of the trail at her feet. Emily took a swig of water, and then poured some into her cupped hand for Lucky. She pulled out the map she'd found at the Ranger's station and studied it.

"Look Lucky," she pointed at a spot on the map and then at the wooden sign with the words, *Lake Lupine Trail -.8 m*, carved into it. "We're more than half way there. I heard some people talking about it at the ranger station last week. They said that if you followed the trail up about three-quarters of the way, you'd reach a place where you can see this cool waterfall through the trees. If you cut in there you can climb the falls the rest of the way to the lake. Said it was totally awesome and much quicker than following the trail."

Lucky cocked her head and wagged her tail raising a cloud of gray dust.

A chipmunk popped up on a rock at the edge of the trail. The little guy stood on his hind legs, like a traffic cop, with his twitching whiskers, raised paws, and alert beady eyes, he scanned his surroundings. Emily recognized him as being a Golden Mantle Ground Squirrel by the stripes on his back. The ranger kept a poster of the alpine wildlife on the wall at the station. Emily spent many hours memorizing it. She wasn't sure whether he saw Lucky first or vice-versa but the instant he saw her he flew from the rock and skittered into the underbrush with Lucky in hot pursuit.

Emily waited a few moments for Lucky to return. When she didn't, Emily called out, "Lucky, here girl." She waited. Growing concerned, she stepped off the trail into the shadows of the dense alpine forest. "Lucky, where are you?" She walked a little further and then stopped to listen. Hearing rustling ahead, she ran towards the sound, pushing past pine boughs and hopping over downed branches and half-buried granite boulders, until she came upon a sunlit clearing thick with Manzanita. Lucky had her nose in the red brush, her tail waving madly. She began digging at the ground in an effort to follow the rodent further into the thicket. She looked up long enough to bark a greeting, and then focused back on the squirrel who was, surely by now, tucked safe and sound in his den.

"Come on, Lucky. Let's go back to the trail. I want to get to the lake before lunchtime. I'm getting hungry already."

Lucky wagged her tail and after one last look at the Manzanita thicket turned to follow Emily.

Emily walked several yards before stopping. She looked around in confusion. "We should have reached the trail by now, girl. I know it wasn't this far. I'm sure we're going the right way...at least I think we are." The beginnings of concern crept through her belly like a spider. She looked at her dog, who sat and returned her gaze. "We just have to think," Emily said.

Lucky waited patiently, allowing Emily to think, but it was no use. After thinking with all her might she was still uncertain how to proceed. She knew that if she were headed in the wrong direction, then walking farther would get them even more lost. And yet, she couldn't stand there and do nothing. Maybe if she could get high enough she would be able to see the trail. She looked for a tree she could climb, but the trees were all either too tall, with their lowest branches out of reach, or too short and wimpy to support her weight. She walked a few yards farther and then stopped. She really didn't know what to do. The spider in her gut multiplied and she suddenly felt ill.

"Come on, Lucky. Let's go over by that rock outcropping and sit for a minute. We can have a drink and something to eat. Maybe that will help us think," Emily said. She found a low smooth rock at the base of a huge granite boulder to sit on and dug into her backpack for her water, granola bar and the bag of dog biscuits. Lucky sat in front of her, eyeing the biscuits. Emily offered Lucky a treat. She carefully peeled back the foil wrapper on her chocolate chip granola bar and took a bite. It tasted great. She really was hungry. Suddenly she had an idea. "We can't be that far from the trail. If we just yell, someone is bound to hear us. There must be lots and lots of hikers besides us."

"Hello?" Emily called. "Can anybody hear me?"

Lucky jumped up and barked.

"Hush, Lucky. I need to hear if someone answers."

Emily listened but could hear nothing except for the squawk of a blue jay, and the 'rat-a-tat-tat' of a woodpecker.

"Hello," she called again. "Is anybody there?"

Emily listened again. Nothing. She suddenly felt very alone. She picked up Lucky and hugged her tight. "We're lost," she whispered into Lucky's fur. "I wonder how long it'll take before Mom even notices we're gone? No one knows where we are. I doubt they could even find us up here if they looked—we're so far from the trail." Her eyes welled with tears and her bottom lip began to quiver. "I wonder if Mom'll even miss us? Probably she and ol' Principal Smelly-Pants will have a tea party."

Emily blinked back tears and looked around one more time, straining to see a hint of the trail through the trees. Seeing nothing, she closed her eyes and leaned back against the boulder. It was warm from the sun and she allowed the warmth to seep through her and melt the icy fear that chilled her heart. "You'd think someone else would be out here hiking today," she said in a small voice. "Someone's got to come by soon. We really messed up. We broke all the wilderness rules. We didn't tell anyone where we were going and we left the trail."

Lucky squirmed and Emily set her down.

"Hey," she said standing. "Maybe if I climb to the top of these rocks I'll be able to see something."

Lucky wagged her tail and stood up on her hind legs.

"No, girl, you can't come. It's too steep for you—dangerous." Emily scrambled up a couple of small boulders but soon reached a giant rock that towered above her. She eyed it critically. It was at least twice her height. There was a huge crack along one side of it that she could use as a foothold and a couple of smaller cracks or gouges that she might use as hand holds. She had gone to the climbing wall at the university with her dad a couple of times. It's not that hard and not even that scary—if you don't look down.

Emily stuck one tennis shoe in the crack and tested her weight to see if it would hold. Her foot hurt a little from being squished, but she was able to lift herself up and find a solid handhold above. Wedging her other foot higher into the same crack, she was able to climb higher, and again even higher. She climbed several feet when the crack began to narrow to the point where she could no longer wedge her foot into it.

Above her and to the right a brittle and twisted pine grew from the granite. Its gnarly roots clenched the rock like skeleton fingers, and its trunk was stunted and bent. It looked sturdy enough to hold her weight if she could only reach it. She stretched out her arm. It was too far. She leaned farther and stretched harder but to no avail. If she could climb a little bit higher and lean over a tiny bit more, she could reach the branch and pull herself up to the top of the rock.

She spotted another possible foothold between her and the tree but doubted it would hold her for long. Shallow and smooth, it was more like a dent in the rock than anything else. She looked at the spot and then down at Lucky. That was a mistake. Her stomach flipped and her head began to spin. She closed her eyes and hugged the rock while she waited for the feeling to pass. Her heart was pounding and the palms of her hands begin to sweat. She concentrated on breathing deeply and soon the merry-go-round slowed, and her stomach settled into place.

She was okay, but not for long. Her arms ached and legs were beginning to tremble. She had to move quickly. She eyed the dent one more time. In one fluid motion she swung herself around, planted her foot, and immediately pushed off, launching herself towards the tree. She grabbed hold of the branch easily and using the roots pulled herself to safety.

She steadied herself on the dome of the giant boulder. Wiping the dusty, scraped palms of her hands on her shorts, she held them up to her forehead and scanned the horizon. She looked straight ahead, then to her right, and then to her right some more, until she came nearly full circle and that's when she saw it. She could see the trail off in the distance, a thin scar on the hillside, and she followed it with her eyes until it dropped from sight behind a ridge. She was able to pick it up again as it crested the ridge and descended into a stand of trees. It seemed to be headed toward her and she strained to see the spot where it came back into view again.

She crept closer and closer to the sheer edge of the tall rock, aware of how near she was getting but desperate to find the trail. She looked down and there it was, right below her, snaking between the stand of trees and the very rock she was standing on. She couldn't believe it. All this time she was searching for the trail, and getting more and more scared, when it was right behind them all along. She breathed a huge sigh of relief. Then she remembered she had to climb back down.

CHAPTER FIFTEEN

Emily was ready to reach the lake. Past ready. She even considered turning back. She'd had enough adventure for one day. Sheer stubbornness kept her going. She was determined to have her picnic on the shores of Lake Lupine if it freakin' killed her. Besides, she had to be almost there—she'd been walking forever. The trail continued through the forest and began to climb. Emily zipped her sweatshirt. While it was warm in the direct sun, it was dark and chilly in the shade beneath the trees.

She heard trickling water and stopped. Turning towards the sound, she stared through the spaces between the trees. Light flickered—the reflection of sun on water. A faint path veered away from the trail and into the woods. Footprints in the dust. Trampled vegetation leading into the trees. Emily felt certain she'd found the shortcut to the waterfall.

She started to follow it. Stopped mid-stride. The last time she'd left the main trail, she and Lucky had almost gotten lost. She turned and looked back at the trail, then forward towards the light. It was like skateboarding. If you always played it safe you never improved, never experienced the thrill of the edge. If she turned back now she'd be just like her mom, who had backed so far away from the edge she couldn't even see it anymore.

Emily marched forward and stepped into the light. A ski slope of granite sparkled with crystalline specks of quartz and fools-gold, like leprechauns had spilled their pots of glimmering coins down the mountainside. Emily knew an ancient landslide had probably caused this sleek, barren scar on the mountain, but she liked the thought of leprechauns better. Best of all, the water slipping, sliding and spilling down the rock face—the waterfall.

"Come on, Lucky, we're almost there."

Emily and Lucky scrambled up the waterfall, mindful of areas slick with slimy green moss or the deeper pools where the water settled. Lucky was Miss Priss when it came to getting her feet wet and she leapt from ledge to ledge in an effort to stay dry. Emily knew wet sneakers could give her blisters but she didn't care. She was having so much fun. Even though she knew they had to hike all the way back later. Even though hiking in the backcountry was a lot tougher than hiking around the woods at home—a lot tougher than she thought it would be.

As she climbed she paused to marvel at how the tiniest little flowers clung tenaciously to cracks in the rock, determined to bloom and grow. She scratched her head in wonder when she saw itty-bitty fish, flashing silver streaks, darting about a shallow pool. How did they get there? What did they find to eat in that puddle of water? Where did they go when they grew too big?

Finally they arrived—the top of the world where lake and waterfall met. It was the most beautiful place on the whole planet. In front of them, the clear pale-blue waters of Lake Lupine, a shallow granite bowl surrounded by windswept miniature pines, ice carved rock formations, and delicate mountain wild flowers.

The lake funneled over a low spot in the stone basin. It could hardly be called a river, because within about ten feet it gently cascaded down the smooth granite face of the waterfall. Emily followed the water's path with her eyes down the very rock she had climbed. She could see Emerald Lake sparkling beyond the mountain peaks, in the distance far below. She couldn't believe they'd walked so far.

Emily raised her arms, threw her head back and shouted. "I am queen of the mountain. Awesome! Totally awesome place for a picnic." She dug into her backpack for Lucky's biscuits and her lunch. She watched with some envy as Lucky bent down and lapped at the clear, cold water of the stream. The water in her bottles had warmed considerably and Emily longed to lie down on her belly and sip from the stream as well, but remembering the parasites, she didn't. *Could they make Lucky sick?* She had tried to give Lucky only bottled water, but early on the dog had decided to drink from each and every watering hole they passed. Emily sighed. *Dr. Soleil will know what to do.* She would stop by the office later and ask him.

Emily took off her damp shoes and set them in the sun to dry. She peeled off her socks, which were dirt colored from the ankle up. The bottoms of her feet burned from all the walking. She decided to dip them in the stream while she ate. Scooting up to the edge, she dunked a heel into the running water. "Yikes," she gasped, "that's cold." She slowly dipped both feet beneath the surface. The snowmelt was so cold her feet hurt and she lifted them out again. She was pretty sure if she kept them in the water any longer they'd become numb, turn blue, and maybe even freeze solid.

She ate her sandwich at the water's edge, dipping her feet until she couldn't stand it, then thawing them on the sun warmed rock. She was ravenous from the hiking. She tucked the empty baggies back into her pack, because she knew the ranger would kill her if she left trash in the wilderness. *Okay,* she admitted, *maybe he wouldn't kill me, but he'd sure lecture me.* Reaching for her orange, she accidentally bumped one of her shoes and it tumbled into the stream.

"Oh, no!" She leaped up and tried to snag it before the water swept it away. Too late. She watched helplessly as the shoe sailed downstream and disappeared over the edge. She tried to follow it down the waterfall, but barefoot she was too slow.

Lucky took off like Mighty Dog. She raced down the hill after the wayward sneaker like she was playing a good game of fetch. She caught up with the shoe easily and returned it to Emily, tail wagging, tongue lolling out the side of her mouth.

"Good girl, Lucky." Emily said, hugging her dog. "That was a close one."

Lucky sat, cocked her head and eyed the shoe expectantly. She wanted to play again and looked disappointed when Emily slipped it on her foot and tied the laces. The shoe was cold and wet but Emily wasn't taking any more chances.

She peeled and ate her orange and rinsed her sticky hands in the stream. She pulled out her field book, and flipped through the pages looking for some of the wild flowers she saw along the way. Reading more of *The Philosopher's Stone* was next on her mental list but she wondered if she should head back instead. She already read it once, but she loved it so much she wanted to read it again, even if the suspense would be gone this time.

Her dad told her a good book was worth reading twice. "You always find new things—things you missed the first time around," he said.

It seemed her dad was usually right about most things—unlike her mother, who hadn't gotten much of anything right since he died.

Emily allowed herself to remember him. His cheek, like sandpaper, when he gave her a goodnight kiss. His hugs—squeezing so tight she thought her ribs would break. His favorite tweed jacket with the leather patches at the elbows that smelled of him and aftershave. How his eyes crinkled when he heard something funny, he'd throw back his head and laugh so hard his belly shook.

Emily stood on top of the mountain where she could see for miles, but her eyes were directed inward. What she saw in the distance was his smiling face. A single tear leaked from the corner of each eye and she angrily wiped them away. "Not fair," she shouted into the wind. She stooped down, picked up a rock and heaved it with all her might. "It's not fair!"

"Come on, Lucky, let's get out of here. We have to get all the way back down this mountain and bike all the way home before it gets dark." She stuffed the orange peel, empty water bottle and remaining biscuits into her backpack.

The main trail rounded the lake before heading back down the mountain. For a moment she considered following it. While climbing up the waterfall had been easy, it looked a lot harder and steeper going down. But the trail would add more distance to her hike and she was already so tired she didn't want to walk any farther than she had to.

Climbing down the waterfall was slow work. Emily tried to keep her feet dry but at times had no choice but to step in the water. Occasionally she climbed down backwards on all fours like she was on a ladder. Sometimes she sat on her rear end and scooted down the rough spots. Once she slipped a little and her butt got soaked.

She was glad those stupid kids from school weren't there to see her. They'd tease her and pretend like she wet her pants. She really hated those bullies. Sometimes she just wished they'd go play on the freeway—during rush hour. Of course there wasn't a freeway near Emerald Lake, but she wished there was, just so they could play on it.

The sheer expanse of the granite waterfall narrowed at the base of the mountain funneling the water into a raging river. The dense forest was neatly divided by the river carved gorge, like the part in her hair. Above the tree line, but near the base of the water fall the rock turned to scree, slivers of granite that had broken loose over the years and slid down hill. It made hiking all the more difficult.

Emily didn't remember having to navigate the scree when she climbed up the waterfall. She began to wonder if she'd missed the shortcut. It was little more than a footpath—easy to miss. She felt that sinking feeling in the pit of her stomach. She was the world's worst hiker. How could she get lost twice in one day? She paused. Shading her eyes with her hand, she scanned the hillside for the trail.

She saw it, up about twenty feet, faint but unmistakable. Relieved, she began to run, leaping from rock to rock. "Come on, Lucky. This way. It's time to go home."

The rock underfoot teetered and wobbled. "Whoa," Emily windmilled her arms struggling to maintain her balance. The rock dislodged and started to slide. Emily leaped to her left as it tumbled down the hillside, scrambing to get a footing on the scree, but it was no use. Emily was sliding down the mountainside.

Digging fingers into the hillside to slow herself, her nails tore as the rock came loose in her hands. The edge of the cliff loomed below and she was approaching it quickly. Screaming, she fell over. She grabbed at the rock once more. This time her hands held. Emily was hanging from the edge by her fingers, her legs swinging in mid-air. Her arms ached and her hands were scraped and raw. She knew she couldn't hold on for long. She looked down and gasped. There was a ledge below, and while it was closer to a ten-foot drop than a hundred, it was still too far to fall. It was going to hurt. Her grasp weakened, then her hands gave way.

CHAPTER SIXTEEN

Emily was lying on her back. Lucky was whining and barking above her. *Why?* Emily opened her eyes and was blinded by the sun. She shaded them with her hand. Where was she? Everything hurt. Her head pounded like she'd been hit by stampeding elephants. Gingerly feeling her scalp she winced when she found a knot. Lucky sounded so far away. Where did she go? "Here, Lucky. Come on, girl," Emily managed to croak before drifting off again.

She awoke to a cold nose nudging her cheek and a slobbering lick to her ear. Lucky whimpered. Emily opened her eyes and found herself nose to nose with her dog. Lucky looked delighted and licked her face.

"Hey girl," Emily ruffled the dog's fur, "what happened? Where are we?" Emily glanced around without moving her head too much.

A wall of granite to her right and to her left—nothing. She was on a ledge maybe four or five feet wide.

It all came back to her. Losing the trail, slipping on the loose rock, tumbling down the mountain, and finally falling. Her heart thumped and she felt light headed. "Pull your self together, Emily Marie Locke," she scolded. "Everything's going to be okay. You're okay. All you have to do is get up and go home."

Emily sat up slowly, fighting dizziness and nausea. Her left leg was killing her. It stuck out at an odd angle and her ankle was twice its usual size. She tried to move it and was instantly sorry. Pain, sharp enough to bring tears, shot up her leg. Emily cried out and fell back in the dirt.

Have to get up. Have to get back before Mom gets home. Gritting her teeth, she sat up again. Fighting waves of darkness she tried to stand but couldn't. Frantically she looked around for a stick to use as a crutch. Nothing. She'd give anything for the one left at the trailhead. *Should have kept it.* Maybe she could scoot backwards on her butt, dragging her legs behind. Pushing with her hands she tried to inch herself back. Agony. Emily couldn't do it. It didn't really matter because she had no idea which way to go. Not only was she hurt—she was lost. *Mom's going to kill me. I'll be grounded for the rest of my life.*

"Help me," Emily screamed. "Somebody please." Her voice was carried away by the wind. The indifferent sounds of rustling leaves and trickling water were her only response. She was in big trouble. Big, big trouble. Bigger trouble than an angry mom.

She shivered as the sun dipped behind the trees. It would be dark soon. No one could hear her. Most likely, her mom didn't know she was gone yet, so nobody was coming. They wouldn't even be looking for her. She was alone.

Lucky whined and licked her paw.

Emily pulled the dog to her. As long as she had Lucky she wasn't completely alone. Together they would be okay. They would make it through the night and in the morning someone would come. Lucky licked her paw again then started chewing at her nails.

"What's the matter, girl?" Emily examined Lucky's front right foot and found a wad of sap stuck between her toes. Lucky tugged at it with her teeth, then shook her head and spit out a gummy chunk. Emily felt the webbing between her toes to make sure it was gone and Lucky flinched. Looking closer she saw a jagged cut across the pad of her foot. "Oh, poor Lucky, you're hurt." She thought of the Band-Aids in her pack. "If we're going to survive the night we need supplies. My backpack," Emily looked around. "Where's my backpack?"

Lucky cocked a brow and glanced in both directions.

"I had it on...." A flash of color in a scraggly bush clinging to the rock above caught her eye. "My backpack! It must have snagged on a branch when I fell." The bag hung several feet above her head. Stretching her arms as high as she could didn't even come close. Maybe if she

123

could pull herself up to a standing position she could reach it. She needed that pack. Finding a handhold in the rock, she tried to pull herself up. Pain in her leg stopped her. It was no use. Giving up, she collapsed in the dirt and started to cry.

A rock dug uncomfortably into her shoulder blade and she shifted her weight. A *rock!* Maybe she could use it to knock the bag loose from the branch. Emily sat up painfully and dug the rock from the soil. It was the size of a goose egg. She felt the weight of it in her hand. Took aim. Threw. It missed her bag by a foot, bounced off the cliff face and clattered down the mountainside. Emily's heart sank. Frantically she looked around for another rock.

She saw one. It was behind her, a foot or so beyond her reach. It wasn't going to come to her—she had to go to it. She scooted backwards a few inches at a time. Each time darkness enveloped. Tears streamed down her cheeks. She needed to rest between each push, to gather the strength and courage to keep trying.

The first star appeared in the sky before she reached the rock—the North Star, bright and low on the horizon. It was the motivation she needed for the final push. Darkness fell quickly in the mountains. She didn't have long before it would be too dark to see her backpack. One more painful push. Lying flat on her back with her arms stretched out above her head she was finally able to touch the rock with her fingertips. Carefully she worked at it, coaxing it towards her. Finally she had it.

She sat up and waited for her world to stop spinning. Her body shook from cold and pain. She willed herself to be still while she took aim. If she missed this time she wouldn't have enough strength to try again. Taking a deep breath she launched the rock and hit the bag square on. Her backpack swung on the branch like a piñata. Just when she thought it wouldn't come down she heard the snap of cracking wood. Her backpack came crashing down and landed with a thump near her good leg.

Emily dug into her bag, found her sweatshirt, and zipped it up to her chin. She was getting colder by the minute. Thirsty, she dug in her pack for a water bottle, discarding an empty one before finding one half full. She took a gulp and then another. She wanted more but decided she should conserve her water. For the first time she considered that it might have to last a long time. Lucky looked at the water longingly, but Emily could still hear the waterfall in the distance. Lucky would have to go there if she needed water. She had three good feet to Emily's one.

She thought she should eat something. All she could find were a couple of dog biscuits. She'd eaten everything she had packed for lunch. Digging into her pack again she came up with the three Band-Aids. She examined her sore hands—scratched, scraped, caked with mud and dried blood. She started to laugh and couldn't stop. She threw the Band-Aids down the mountainside. "That's right Ranger Stranger—I'm a litterbug," she yelled. Then her laughter dissolved into hiccups, and she allowed herself to feel very sorry for herself, but only for a minute. Her pack was the one she used for school. Maybe there was still something buried in the bottom of a pocket? Emily searched and found a half eaten cookie in a baggie and two sour balls wrapped in plastic that were just a little gooey. She ate the cookie not knowing or caring if eating a three-month old cookie could make her sick. She licked the crumbs off her grubby fingers and then turned the baggie inside out and licked it. Unwrapping both candies, she stuffed them into her mouth at the same time.

Lucky hadn't taken her eyes off the biscuits since Emily had found them. "You haven't had your dinner either, girl," she said, sounding like her mouth was full of marbles. She fed Lucky the last of the dog treats. "Looks like we're both going to lose weight tonight."

Exhausted from both pain and the effort to get her pack, Emily lay back down. Her fingers hurt from the cold. She pulled the cuffs of her sweatshirt down over her hands. She wanted to curl up in a ball to stay warm but couldn't move her leg, which was now totally numb. Her body shook uncontrollably and her teeth clattered. Thank goodness the stars provided faint light so she could make out her surroundings in the dark. She tried counting the stars but kept losing track and getting confused. She felt odd—like she was floating. Floating among the stars. *Second star to the right and straight on till morning*, said the little boy who would never grow up.

She felt the weight of a blanket, soft and furry, settle over her chest. She opened her eyes. Princess Diana was kneeling over her with a halo of stars that sparkled like diamonds. She was so beautiful. The Princess smiled but her big blue eyes seemed sad. Tenderly she brushed the hair off Emily's forehead. Leaning close she started to sing in Emily's ear. "Hush little baby, don't you cry. Mama's going to sing you a lullaby...."

CHAPTER SEVENTEEN

Dr. Ben Soleil was pouring over the books in his office when his phone rang. He looked at it with annoyance. Another interruption. He'd never get the blasted books reconciled. He considered not answering. It was with great reluctance he picked up the handset. It could be an emergency.

"No, Emily's not here, Diana. I haven't seen her all day." He shook his head, leaned back in his chair and rubbed his eyes while he listened. "Did you check the ranger station...the dock? All right, calm down." He could hear Diana Locke becoming more agitated by the minute. Panic was setting in. "I'm sure she's out playing with Lucky and lost track of time. There has to be a reasonable explanation," he assured her. "Is everything okay between you two? Did you two have a fight?" He listened to Diana, the pitch of her voice rising with every word. Her concern was infectious. He began to feel worry's grip on his gut. "Okay. All right. I'll be right there. Let me call the station and see if Wade can meet us at your house."

Ben leapt up the steps to the Dew Drop Inn. Just as he was about to knock the door flew open. Diana stood in the doorway, her face expectant. Her expression fell when she saw him, instead of her daughter, on the front stoop.

"Anything?" he asked, stepping into the entry.

"No." She shook her head and blinked back tears. "Something's happened. I can feel it."

"You don't know anything. Don't borrow trouble. You said Emily was grumpy this morning. Maybe she's just trying to scare you."

Diana's eyes searched his and he realized that she was grasping at any bit of hope to keep her afloat.

"Maybe you're right." She nodded. "She was annoyed with me because I was too busy to spend the day with her. I'm a terrible mother." Her eyes filled again. "I really am."

"You're not...." Her tears made him uncomfortable. He pulled her to him and awkwardly patted her on the shoulder. "You've had a tough time. Doing the best you can. Emily loves you."

She pulled away from him. Gave him that anguished look. A knock at the door filled her eyes with hope again. She flung open the door and the ranger, Wade Carson, stepped in.

"I talked to the sheriff's office and called the hospital before I came," he said, peeling off his coat. "Nothing. I can organize a search party but it'll take me a while. It'll be dark by then."

Diana gasped and wrapped her arms around her stomach. "We have to find her now...I'll go crazy if I have to wait...she'll be scared..."

"I'm telling you that I'll get a search party together. We'll find her," he explained patiently, like he was speaking to a three year old. "It would help if we knew where to start looking. Look around, Diana. Is there anything you can tell me that would give us a clue? What was she wearing? When she was last here? Did she eat lunch? Watch TV? Read a book? Did she take anything with her? Her skateboard?"

Diana's eyes flew to the shelf in the corner where Emily kept her board. She pointed. "Her board is here."

All heads turned towards the board. Emily the Strange and her little black cat were shellacked to the bottom. The dark haired girl looked bemused, like she knew a secret and wasn't telling.

Dr. Ben was relieved. The moment Wade mentioned the board he thought of how often he'd seen Emily riding it in traffic or racing down the hill to the lake. How many times had he warned her to be careful? His mind flashed on the image of her having a run-in with a car...and losing, and he felt sick. He breathed deeply. *She's not on her skateboard. But where is she?* He looked out the window. Dusk—less than an hour of light left.

"The sheriff," Wade continued," he's got two guys out in cruisers. Told them to keep their eyes open. Let us know if they see anything."

Someone else knocked. Diana raced to the door and opened it. Again her face collapsed.

Amber stood at the door clutching a Barbie in one hand. "Can Emily play?" She asked.

"No," Diana said and started to shut the door.

"I wanted to go with her this morning but I had to go shopping with my mom."

Stunned, Diana pulled the door back open.

Amber suddenly found herself looking into the faces of all three adults. She had their full attention. "What?" she asked.

"Where is she," Diana cried.

"Let me handle it," Wade said. "Come in, Amber. Sit down and tell us what you're talking about. Where was Emily going this morning?"

"Hiking. She had her backpack out. Food. And this book she told me about."

"Think, Amber. Did she tell you where she going hiking?"

Amber scrunched up her face. "A lake. She heard people talk about it at the ranger station. She said it was a long way—that I couldn't walk that far. But I could. I know I could."

Ben Soleil, Wade Carson and Diana Locke looked at each other and then back at Amber.

"Sweetie, did she tell you the name of the lake?" Diana's voice was pleading.

"Maybe." Amber looked at each of them in turn. She shook her head. "I don't remember."

The walkie-talkie, clipped to the ranger's belt, crackled with static. Raising it to his ear, he pushed a button and said, "Wade here. Talk to me." His brow furrowed. He looked at the others. "The deputies found a bicycle with a basket attached to the handlebars at the trailhead to the Desolation Wilderness area."

"Yes, that's Emily's. Oh, thank God," Diana said. "Let's go get her."

"It's not that easy," the ranger said.

Diana's expression darkened. "The lake...."

"There are dozens of lakes up there. It'll be dark soon. We can't search the wilderness in the dark."

"But, my baby...." Diana looked to Ben for support. "We can't just leave her."

"They're checking the immediate area now. Maybe she's on her way down the trail and she'll show up any minute." The radio crackled again. Wade listened. Shook his head. "They just talked to some hikers coming off the trail—it continues nearly a mile up the mountain before it splits—said they didn't see anyone else on it. I'm going back to the office and get that search party organized for the morning. We'll meet at dawn at the trailhead."

Diana collapsed in a chair. "No."

"I'm sorry. It's too dangerous at night."

CHAPTER EIGHTEEN

The words of the song drifted through Emily's consciousness. *And if that mocking bird don't sing, Mama's gonna buy you a diamond ring.* But the bird was singing. She could hear it. Not singing. Squawking. Not a mockingbird, more like a Blue Jay. As the fog in Emily's brain lifted she could hear the sounds around her, chirping birds, rustling trees and trickling water—nature's song. Where was she? Not in her own bed— that's for sure. She became aware of the cold, the numbness in her limbs and the weight on her chest.

She heard a soft rumble in her ear. The kind of sound a wild animal might make. *Lions and tigers and bears. Oh no!* Holding her breath, afraid to move—not that she could if she wanted—she opened her eyes and peered down past her nose. Lucky was asleep on her chest, sprawled spread eagle, snoring softly in her ear.

Emily raised leaden arms and hugged her dog.

Instantly awake, Lucky licked her face, then squirmed out of her arms, walked a few feet and squatted to pee. After what seemed to Emily like a long time, she finished and returned. Sitting by Emily's shoulder, the dog stared down into her face and waited. Waited for Emily to tell her what to do. Waited for Emily to save them.

Emily turned her face away. She couldn't save them. Couldn't even move. *Poor Lucky is the unluckiest dog in the world to be stuck with me*, Emily thought. She could feel a tear spill from the corner of her eye, run down her face and puddle in her ear.

Lucky leaned over and licked the tears from her face.

"I'm sorry, girl. Sorry I got you into this trouble. And I'm tired, so very tired, and so very, very cold." Sometime during the night the cold had settled deep in her bones and she'd stopped shivering "Maybe Dad will know what to do, Lucky. He always knows what to do." Emily whispered as her eyes fluttered shut.

CHAPTER NINETEEN

Dr. Ben Soleil pulled his Land Rover into Diana's driveway at five A.M. sharp. Before he'd come to a complete stop, Diana was halfway to the car. He leaned across the passenger seat and pushed open the door for her. She climbed in without saying a word and fastened her seatbelt. Even in the pre-dawn darkness he could see the dark hollows that had settled around her eyes and the tension in her neck and jaw. He handed her a steaming cup of coffee. Had he looked away, for even a second, he would have missed the smile of gratitude that flickered across her face before the solemn mask of fear returned.

"Did you get any sleep?" he asked. One look at her told him she hadn't. He'd almost offered to spend the night on her couch for moral support, but he'd felt awkward about it. Truthfully, although he was close to Emily, he didn't know her mother all that well. In fact, after the fiasco at Emily's birthday party he'd pretty much avoided her. Only spoke to her if he had to, like when she came to his office looking for Emily or if they ran into each other at the market. He didn't even like Diana Locke much. Although he had to admit that lately she seemed better, since she'd quit drinking and started therapy. He was beginning to see the woman she must have been before life had dumped a heap-load of garbage on her. Even now, in all her fear and desperation, her defenses down, he felt her strength of spirit. If he'd ever doubted Diana's love for Emily, he didn't any more.

The trailhead parking lot was filled to capacity. At least a dozen people, visible in the headlights, clustered around the ranger's truck. Ben had to park on the side of the road beyond the lot.

Diana's eyes widened as they drove slowly past the gathering crowd. "Oh... All these people...here to help...." She recognized neighbors, customers from Johnston's store, and friends from her support group. The ranger's son, Tyler Carson, stood next to his dad along with another teenage boy she recognized from Emily's bus stop. After feeling so alone the past year she was overwhelmed. Now, in her darkest hour, she felt a real sense of community. These people were here for Emily, and for her.

A map of the wilderness was spread out on the tailgate of the ranger's truck. Several people gathered around Wade Carson who had a flashlight in one hand and a pencil, which he used as a pointer, in the other. "This here," he indicated a gently curving line, "is the trail." He pointed the flashlight in the direction of the trailhead, which was still buried in darkness. "It passes through this grove of Aspens and then across a meadow before it starts to climb up the mountain." He followed the line on the map with his pencil to the point where it started to zig-zag. "We'll all go up this together. When we get here," he tapped a spot a few inches higher on the map, "the trail splits. We'll break into three groups. The first group will follow the fork to the right to Lupine Lake. It continues on from there, but I doubt she could have made it any further than that—if she even made it that far. The other two groups will take the split to the left. In about a quarter of a mile it splits again. One group will go towards Lake Edward and the other group will continue towards the lower and upper Twin Lakes. Check the area closely looking for any sign she might have gone that way. Call in on the walkie-talkie immediately if you see anything.

The people nodded and started breaking up into groups.

"Ben, you stay here with Diana," Wade said.

"What?" Ben said. "No. I want to help."

The ranger rested a hand on Ben's shoulder. "That would be helping," he said.

"Why me? I need to be looking for Emily. I need to help find her," Ben said. "All I could think of last night was her up here alone...."

Wade pulled Ben aside. "Stay with Diana. You know her. She needs someone she trusts right now to be with her."

"I know Emily. Diana's just her mom—I don't really know her that well...."

"Please, Ben. I understand your feelings, but I need you to do this...."

Ben Soleil kicked the dirt in frustration. "Okay." It was hard to sit back and do nothing. He'd grown pretty fond of Emily ever since she showed up at his door with that goofy dog of hers smelling like skunk. He wanted to be the one who rescued her.

Ben and Diana watched as Wade led the groups up the trail at first light. Ben suggested they wait in the truck where it would be warmer. He was concerned about Diana. She looked frightened and vulnerable. Wrapping a blanket around her, he poured another cup of coffee from a thermos, handed it to her and sat back to wait.

CHAPTER TWENTY

Emily struggled to wake up. She felt weak and thick-headed, like she'd been slogging through mental quicksand. Other than the weight on her chest, she couldn't feel her body. Lucky had crawled on top of her again, her head resting on Emily's neck. Emily coughed. Looked for her water bottle. Surprised to find she was holding it. Opening the bottle, she lifted it to her lips with a wooden arm and downed the last sip.

"Lucky." Emily wrapped her fingers in the dogs fur and pulled her muzzle close. "This is really bad. I'm in real trouble. You have to go." She enunciated slowly. "Go...find...help. Do you understand?"

Lucky whined and pulled away.

"No, Lucky. You have to." Emily pushed the dog away from her and pointed down the mountain.

Lucky lay down on her haunches and crept back towards Emily.

"Go, Lucky. Go! Get help!" Emily picked up the empty water bottle and threw it at her dog.

Lucky dodged the bottle, cocked her head and looked at Emily, then looked around her. The ledge wrapped around the rock face where it met the scree rockslide, and beyond it the edge of the forest. Lucky lowered her head, tucked her tail between her legs and slinked away. After about five yards she stopped and looked back once more, her brown eyes sad and fearful.

"Go!" Emily pleaded, as she fought the darkness that hovered over her like a shroud.

CHAPTER
TWENTY-ONE

*B*en stretched and breathed deeply of the pine-scented air. After a second cup of coffee he'd excused himself to use the restroom—which was a fancy name for the stinky, buggy, hole in the ground, outhouse at the base of the trail. *But when you gotta go, you gotta go.*

Diana sat in the car clutching the blanket around her. In an effort to pass the time he'd tried to talk with her, but she was too frightened to hold a coherent thought much less a conversation. He soon gave up and they sat entombed in silence.

Thinking he saw a movement in the trees, he froze and held his breath. Squinting, he searched the woods. *Is it a squirrel? Branches moving in the breeze? There it is again. It looks like...a fox... maybe a raccoon. It's Lucky!*

Ben could see her favoring a front paw as she trotted down the trail towards him. "Diana, come quickly...." he called as he ran towards Emily's dog. Lucky's tongue hung from the side of her mouth. She'd been running hard. He knelt down to pick her up, but she backed out of his reach and barked sharply.

"Come here, Lucky," he said.

This time she allowed him to pick her up. She licked his face. When he turned to show her to Diana, who had come running, Lucky squirmed in his arms until he nearly dropped her and barked at him again.

"What?" he said. "What is it, girl? Where's Emily?"

Lucky turned, ran a few feet up the trail, then stopped, turned and barked again at Ben.

"I think she wants me to follow her."

"Let's go," Diana said.

"Let's? But, I promised Wade we'd stay here."

"I'm going, with or without you. I can't just sit here anymore. She's my daughter."

He grasped Diana's shoulders firmly with both hands. "She is your daughter and you need to be here when she comes down this mountain. I'll follow Lucky."

"But...." Diana chewed her bottom lip.

"And frankly, Diana,"—he looked pointedly at her thin soled leather shoes—"I'll be much faster on my own."

"Okay. Go!" Diana said. "Quickly."

Ben ran after Lucky, following her up the trail, through the aspen and the meadow thick with wildflowers. Soon the path turned rugged, steeper and harder to climb. Breathing hard, Ben was forced to slow his pace even though he was desperate to keep up with the scraggly black dog. He was increasingly convinced that Lucky was taking him to Emily. She stayed ahead of him, looking back over her shoulder often to make sure he was still there. She waited until he'd nearly catch up, her little chest huffing and puffing from exertion, then she'd turn and run on.

When they reached the fork in the trail Lucky headed to the right towards Lupine Lake. He followed and soon they met the group of men from the returning search party.

"Did you find her?" he asked.

"She's not there. We looked all over. Called her name. No trace. You're heading the wrong way."

"No, Lucky knows where she's going. I'm sure of it."

"I'm telling you, man, we walked completely around the lake, called her name dozens of times, searched for any trace...she's not there."

Lucky barked at Ben impatiently. She turned ran a few more feet then looked back to see if he was coming.

"I'm going this way," he told the men. "Tell Wade...."

"Tell him yourself." The man handed Ben the walkie-talkie. "Take this and let us know if you find anything. Ranger wants us to take a closer look around the bridge, where it crosses over the ravine." The men headed down the trail.

The rising sun had finally crested the mountain-tops casting long shadows on the trail. Ben's shirt was soaked with sweat and his pant legs were damp from the dew that clung to clumps of grass and wild flowers. Even though he was warm from running, he found it quite chilly in the shade. Poor Emily...did she have a jacket with her? He was focused on climbing over some tree roots when he looked up and realized that Lucky had disappeared from sight. Confused, he stopped. Could he possibly have passed her? Bending at the waist to catch his breath he scanned the trail ahead of him, then turned back and checked where he had been. No, no dog in sight.

He called, "Lucky? Where are you?" Listening intently he heard scampering sounds in the brush on the right. He looked into the forest but saw nothing. "Lucky?" he called again. A ray of sun-light flashed on her wet snout, and he finally saw her, camouflaged by the wooded shadows.

Confident he had seen her, Lucky turned and disappeared back into the darkness, untouched by the morning's early light.

Carefully examining the ground in the direction she had gone Ben discovered a faint footpath and followed it. Fifty yards ahead, just when he was ready to give up and retrace his steps, he entered a clearing. He was standing at the edge of a granite hill, at least eight stories tall, with water cascading down the gentle slope of its face. He stood in awe of such unexpected beauty, momentarily forgetting why he was there.

Lucky reminded him. She barked at him and trotted down the hill. He studied the hillside for a sign of Emily. The water from the fall angled off to the left towards a ravine that disappeared into the woods beyond. The base of the hillside appeared to be one big rock pile formed from years, perhaps centuries, of the granite chipping and cracking into loose slivers that tumbled downhill into a pile at the bottom. It looked like treacherous footing and Lucky was headed straight for it. He followed her carefully, slowing significantly once he reached the scree. Slipping and sliding with every step, he considered turning back, radioing Wade, waiting for help. But Emily was out here. Somewhere. Alone. He had to find her.

Ahead of him, a ledge of rock jutted out from the rubble—a boulder the size of a two-story house diagonally buried in the rockslide. He wondered if he could reach it with out sliding down the hillside and falling over. It would be a good vantage point for him to look for Emily. He sidled down towards the cliff, allowing his right foot to grab hold before bringing down his left. It was a painfully slow process. His quads burned from the effort. Every step left him more convinced that Emily could not have come this way. It was too difficult. Too dangerous.

For the first time he doubted the wisdom of following Lucky, who was just a dog after all. What was I thinking? He wondered. This is crazy.

The wilderness is too big—big enough to swallow a little girl without a trace. About eight feet above the cliff face his foot slipped and he started to fall. Leaning into the hillside, he dug in with his heels and managed to stop the downward motion. He tore the elbow of his jacket on a jagged rock and he could feel pain where he'd torn skin underneath too. His right ankle was beginning to talk to him.

"Lucky," he called. "Come here."

The dog was slowly picking her way down the rockslide to the left of the cliff. She turned to look at him and wagged her tail.

"Come on girl, let's go back. She's not here." Looking up the hill, he searched for an easier way back. Maybe if he just crabbed sideways on all fours, like one might swim sideways to get out of a riptide, he could get off the scree. "Come, Lucky."

Lucky freaked. She raced towards him, leaping from rock to rock until she reached the ledge. Standing defiantly, she barked at him. Sharp, demanding, earsplitting, she barked and barked.

"Darn dog," he muttered. "Now I'm going to have to rescue you too." Using his hands and feet, he carefully inched his way towards the cliff. When he finally reached it Lucky wagged her tail and jumped up on his leg with her front paws. Leaning over to pick her up he caught a glimpse of color below—Emily's backpack. Then he saw her, Emily, her limp body lying still on the ledge below.

"Emily!" he called.

She didn't move.

Unclipping the walkie-talkie from his belt and holding it to his mouth, he pressed the button. "Wade, I found her. Can you hear me? Repeat. I have found Emily." His voice cracked with emotion. He swallowed hard and continued, "Come quickly. She needs help... the bottom of a slide area...below Lake Lupine...I'm climbing...down to her...right now. Bring help."

The handset hissed with static and Wade's voice came over loud and clear. "Is she okay, Ben?"

"I think she's hurt. She's not moving."

Then Wade whispered, "Is she alive?"

"I don't know."

CHAPTER
TWENTY-TWO

*D*ing...ding...ding, ba-bump...ba-bump, swish....
Emily slowly became aware of the sounds around
her. Discordant sounds. Like sixth grade band
practice. Hospital sounds. A machine beeping.
A cart rolling on a tiled floor. The swish of a curtain
being pulled back. *What am I doing in a hospital?*

"I think she's waking up. Come quickly,"
someone whispered.

Emily's eyes fluttered as memories swept over
her like bits and pieces of a puzzle she couldn't
quite put together.

"Lucky!" she cried, opening her eyes. Faces
peered down at her, *Mom, Dr. Soleil, the ranger,
Amber and Ryan.* Her heart broke and she began
to sob. "No!" she cried.

151

"What's the matter, honey?" Her mother looked alarmed.

"Lucky. That's why you're all here isn't it? Something's happened to Lucky."

"No."

"Yes, she was hurt. Princess Diana came—"

"Princess Diana? What are you talking about? Princess Diana died last year. Car accident. Remember, honey?"

"She kept me warm," Emily said.

"No, Lucky kept you warm," Dr. Soleil said. He reached for her bandaged hand and held it in his.

"Princess Diana came for Lucky, didn't she?"

"No, Emily." The vet shook his head. "Lucky's fine. She saved your life. She slept on your chest and kept you warm. She came and found us. Led us to you. Really, she's fine."

Emily didn't believe them. "Where is she then?"

"They don't allow dogs in the hospital, Emily," her mother said. "She's at the house."

Emily tried to sit up. "You know, Mary, Queen of Scots...you know, like my middle name—she loved dogs. Her dog curled itself around her feet while she knelt at the block and they chopped off her head..."

"Emily!" Her mother sounded exasperated. "The things that come out of your mouth. You sound just like your dad."

"And he died right after she did."

"Who died?"

"Queen Mary's dog."

"Nobody's dying, Emily. You're fine and so is Lucky," her mom said.

A nurse came in and adjusted a fluid filled bag that hung from a metal pole. "This might make you a little sleepy," she said.

"Lucky hurt her foot," Emily said.

"I told you, she's okay," her mom insisted. "Doctor Soleil cleaned her up and soaked and bandaged her foot. She's going to be good as new."

Her mom sat on the side of the bed and gently brushed the hair from Emily' forehead. "You gave me a good scare, young lady," she said sternly. "You gave all these people a scare."

"Sorry," Emily demurred. Her memory was returning in huge, frightening flashes—the rocks, the cliff, and her leg. She looked towards the foot of the bed. Her leg was in a cast from her foot to her thigh. Her throat tightened and she blinked back tears. She was too proud to admit that she'd given herself a good scare, too.

"I wasn't worried," Amber said. She stepped up to the bed. "You're so smart. You're the smartest person I know. I knew you'd be okay. Here." She held out a wrapped package. "I brought you something. Want me to open it for you? It's a book. I know you like to read."

Emily laughed. "Thanks, Amber." As she watched Amber tear the wrapping off the package, her eyes began to feel heavy.

Amber held up a copy of R. L. Stine's, Goosbumps book, *Brain Juice*.

Emily reached for it. "Thanks Amber, I love these books." Stifling a yawn, she added, "How did you know?"

Amber grinned and shrugged, "I just knew."

Emily tried to read the words on the back cover of the book but her eyes blurred. She fought to keep them open, but was overcome by a numbing weariness. Blinking several times, she whispered, "Mom? So tired...."

"I'm not going anywhere, honey. Get some rest."

When Emily awoke again the sun was low in the sky and cast an orange glow about the room.

"Where is everybody?" she asked.

"They all went home," her mother replied. "You've been asleep for hours."

"What about you? Are you going too?"

"No, honey, I'm not going anywhere. I'm staying right here by your side until they let you out of here."

"What about your work and your meetings?"

"Not important, Emily. You're the most important thing in the world to me, and I'm sorry it took something like this to remind me."

"I bet he's with her right now," Emily said.

"Who?" her mom asked.

"Dad. I bet he's with Princess Diana—you know, hanging out."

"He'd like that," her mom said, smiling. "He's probably lecturing her on British Royalty."

"Yeah, and she's showing him which fork to use for the fish from a place setting with a dozen forks, knives and spoons."

"Maybe they're bowling," her mom suggested.

"She'd win." Emily laughed. "Dad's a terrible bowler."

"I miss him."

"Dad probably sent her to me when I was on the cliff. She sang to me and I wasn't so scared. I like to think of him being with her while he waits for us and she waits for her real Prince Charming." Emily looked down at the cast on her leg. It was starting to itch way down deep inside.

"They're going to get you up to walk on that thing in the morning. Think you're up for that?"

Emily nodded.

"And they're going to give you a lesson on using crutches."

Emily grinned. She'd seen kids at school with crutches before. It always looked like fun. She had sometimes secretly wished something would happen to her so she'd be able to try them.

"And when we get home we're going to have a cast signing party," her mom said. "Invite all your friends. It'll be fun."

Ba-bump, ba-bump, ba-bump...the meal cart stopped outside her room.

An orderly brought in a tray. He said, "Well, look who's up. This is the first time I've seen you with your eyes open, kiddo. You hungry?"

"Are you kidding? I could eat an elephant."

"Yikes! I'll tell you what, I'll look around and see if I can find a second dessert," the order said with a wink. "And while I'm doing tha you might want to take a look out the window Nurse Ratchet just got a call saying you had c visitor." He moved to the window and pulled the curtains wide. He motioned at someone standing outside.

Emily leaned forward expectantly. Dr. Soleil stood in the flowerbed outside her window. He waved then bent down, disappearing from her view. When he stood up, he was holding Lucky in his arms for her to see.

"Lucky, you're okay," she cried. She turned to her mom, "Can she come in, just for a minute? Pleaseeeee?"

"No, Emily. You know the rules. We just thought you'd like to see her. Wave good-bye now. Dr. Soleil will take her home. He's keeping her at the clinic tonight."

Emily waved and kept waving until they disappeared from sight.

Emily's mom removed the cover from her dinner plate and tore the foil lid off a cup of juice. "I ordered for you, I picked all your favorites."

Emily dug her fork into a steaming, creamy, bowl of macaroni and cheese.

"By the way, I have news," her mother said.

"Ummm." Emily licked her fork and filled it again. It tasted so good.

"I got a new job," her mom said.

"You did? Where? Doing what? When did this happen?" Emily mumbled through a full mouth.

Her mother laughed, "One question at a time. Being around here"—she made a hand gesture than encompassed more than just the room—"made me realize I miss my work."

"You got a job here?" Emily's eyes widened.

"No, no...I'm not ready to go back to a hospital yet, but I miss nursing."

"I don't get it," Emily said.

"Karen, Ben's...I...uh...mean Dr. Soleil's nurse, is going on maternity leave next week and with two kids at home, she's not sure she's coming back."

"Yeah, so?"

"So...I'm a nurse. I'm taking her job."

"But...but...but...he's a vet. What do you know about animals?"

"Surgery's surgery and shots are shots—animal or human. How hard can it be? Besides, Ben'll help me. I'm a quick study, I learn fast."

"Ben? Hummm" Emily stabbed a chunk of melon with her fork. "When did you start calling him Ben?"

"You know, he saved your life."

"He said Lucky did."

"Lucky kept you warm until Ben got there." Diana's eyes welled with tears and she reached for a tissue. "After he found you, he worked on you until they could get you out of there. He had medical gear in his backpack...just in case. He warmed you up, stabilized your leg and started an IV all before the medics got there."

"But, he's a veterinarian." Emily laughed. "I'm not a dog."

"Vets are doctors, Emily. Animal or human—it doesn't matter. He's a good doctor and a good man."

Emily couldn't believe her eyes. Her mother was blushing.

CHAPTER TWENTY—THREE

Emily's mother held open the door to the clinic and stood aside as Emily hobbled through on her crutches. She had just gotten out of the hospital. It felt great, although the crutches weren't nearly as much fun as they looked.

"Surprise!" everyone yelled.

"I have markers!" Karen held up three boxes of new, brightly colored marking pens. She walked like a duck and looked like she swallowed a beach ball. "Who wants to be first?"

"I do!" Emily's mom said. She picked a red marker. "Sit down, honey," she said, "while I create my masterpiece." She drew a big red heart with an arrow sticking through it and wrote the words, *Love Mom*, in the middle.

Meanwhile everyone else started picking colors.

Amber drew Ariel, the mermaid—at least that's who she said it was—while Ryan filled in with fish and crabs.

Tyler wrote his name in big, bold, angular letters that reminded her of graffiti she'd seen near the railroad tracks in the city. "Pretty exciting adventure you had there," he said, his eyes filled with admiration. "You're pretty tough...for a girl."

Missy walked in with a giant cookie that said, *Welcome Home, Emily* on it in pink frosting. "I have ice cream too," she said. "Who wants some?"

The ranger plucked a kelly green marker from the box. "My turn," he said. "Hey, Tyler, make yourself useful and get Emily a piece of that cookie and some ice cream. And while you're at it—get a piece for your old man as well."

"Sure, Dad." Tyler winked at Emily.

"What are you drawing?" Emily asked.

The Ranger angled his body in such a way to prevent Emily from seeing what he was coloring on her cast. "You'll see." He worked for a minute more then sat back and said, "Ta da!"

Emily leaned forward. The Ranger had drawn a four-leaf clover on her cast just above the ankle.

"It's a lucky four-leaf clover," he said. "It's to remind you that sometimes it's better to be lucky than good. And you, my dear, were very, very lucky." He smiled at her, then called over his shoulder, "Tyler, what's taking so long?"

Emily thought about what he said. Yes, she'd been lucky and very, very stupid. "Speaking of lucky...wait a minute." She looked around. "Where is Lucky? Mom, why didn't you bring her? I want to see her."

The room fell silent. Everyone looked at each other, but not at her.

Dr. Soleil cleared his throat and nodded at Emily's mother.

Emily's mom knelt on the floor and reached for her hand. "I'm sorry to tell you this, sweetie. Lucky is gone."

"Gone? What do you mean, gone? Gone where?"

"I was going to wait until after the party...." her mom said. She turned to the others. "Can you guys give us a minute?"

Missy picked up the cookie. "Okay, everybody, ice cream and cookie out back on the picnic table," she said leading the way.

"I came home from visiting you at the hospital Tuesday and she was gone. I looked everywhere for her. Called Ben. Talked to the sheriff. Everybody's looking for her."

"But...." Emily felt her world turn upside down.

"We'll find her. I promise," her mother said. "We'll make flyers and put them up all over town. Somebody has to have seen her. I'm sure she'll show up."

Emily's eyes filled with tears. "Maybe it's my fault. Maybe she's out looking for me because I was in the hospital so long. Maybe she's lost... all alone and scared. We have to go now, Mom. We have to find her."

CHAPTER
TWENTY-FOUR

The doors of the school bus opened with a whoosh and Emily climbed off. There was a chill in the air. She shivered and zipped her jacket up to her chin. With shoulders hunched and hands in her pockets she walked past a stand of Aspens. The wind turned and bright yellow leaves showered down on her. She reached the veterinary clinic but rather than go inside to check in with her mom she decided to sit on the steps for a while. Dr. Soleil must have seen her from the window. He came out, buttoned his jacket, and sat down next to her.

Without looking up Emily said, "Emily Bronte once told the kids at school that her dog meant more to her than they did."

"She must have had a great dog," Dr. Soleil said.

"Yeah...and sometimes the kids at school are jerks."

"Bad day?" he asked.

"No." Emily looked at him. "I just miss Lucky so much. She was my best friend."

"Yes, she was a great dog." He wrapped an arm around her and pulled her close.

"I don't understand," Emily said. "What happened to her? Where did she go?"

"I guess we'll never know. We looked everywhere. She just disappeared," he said. "Sometimes we lose loved ones and we don't know why. What's important is remembering the good times you spent together and the love you shared."

They sat in silence for a couple of minutes. Emily thought about Lucky and the bees...Lucky and the skunk...Lucky and the fishhook. Then her thoughts of Lucky morphed into memories of her dad.

Ben said, "Lucky came into your life at a time when you needed her. Maybe she decided you were okay now—you didn't need her any more. Maybe she went off to find some other kid who did." He picked a yellow leaf from Emily's hair. "At least that's what I like to think happened to her."

Emily nodded, her eyes brimming with tears. "Yeah, maybe that's what happened...except I still do need her," she sniffed loudly and wiped her nose on her sleeve.

"Did you decide what you're going to be for Halloween?" he asked.

"Yeah." She grinned through her tears, "I think I'm going to dress up like Emily The Strange. I need a long, black wig, a black dress and a pair of white Mary Janes."

"And a black cat?"

"Yeah, I have a stuffed animal that's a black cat, and I think mom has a black dress I can wear."

"Great. I'm sure all the cool kids will know who you are, even if their parents don't."

Emily smiled and shrugged. "Yeah...parents are clueless."

The vet cleared his throat. "Look, Emily...your mom and I want to talk to you."

Talk? Oh, no, she thought. Her mother and... Ben—he told her to call him Ben—had been getting awfully chummy since her mom started working at the clinic. Emily had seen the way they were looking at each other. Seen them with their heads together, talking quietly, or laughing at some shared joke. It was kind of weird but it was okay. Emily liked him. Her mom liked him. Her mom was happy again for the first time since her Dad died. And, Emily was happy again, too.

Things were better at home and at school. She'd started the school year on crutches. Found that the story of her *wilderness adventure* had made the rounds like skaters at the roller-rink. She was a celebrity. And while she cared little for the notoriety, it had given her an inroad to making friends in this small town. Things were better—except Lucky. She still felt a sadness inside that could trigger instant tears when she thought of her missing dog. Just like for her dad.

"What did you want to talk to me about?" she asked.

"Emily, when you lose someone you love, you can't just replace them."

Emily looked into his eyes.

"But our hearts are huge," Ben said. " We have enough room in them to love again and again, even while still loving those who are gone. Do you understand?"

Emily nodded uncertainly. "What are you trying to say?"

"Come on in so your mom can tell you too." Ben stood up and offered Emily a hand.

Reluctantly she followed him indoors, not sure she was ready for whatever they wanted to tell her.

Her mother came into the waiting room, blinked at Emily, checked her watch and said, "Oh, hi. Is it after four already? Where does the time go?" She was wearing a white lab coat and her hair was pulled back. She walked over to Ben and slipped her hand into his.

"What is it?" Emily looked from one to the other.

Ben smiled at her mom and said, "You tell her."

"Somebody better tell me quickly or I'm going to explode," Emily said.

"Okay, Emily," her mother said. "We wanted to tell you...I mean, Ben thought it would be a good idea...."

"What? Just tell me."

"We got a litter of puppies in today. Their owner couldn't keep them. So we thought that you could take care of them. Get to know them. And when they're old enough you can have your pick of the litter."

"Puppies?" Emily gasped.

"Sure, what did you think we were talking about?" her mother asked.

"As I was trying to tell you outside," Ben said, "your new puppy won't be Lucky. It could never replace her. Lucky was a very special dog and you loved her very much. But you'll love this new puppy, too. You'll see."

"Puppies?" Emily's head was spinning. "Really? I can have one? Where are they? Let me see them." She hugged her mom and Dr. Soleil, both at the same time, then raced to the boarding room where they always kept the puppies.

In the whelping box in the corner were six squirming balls of fur. They had bright, shiny eyes, long floppy ears and square snouts. Two were reddish brown, one black with odd pale green eyes, and the other three were tri-colored. Emily climbed into the box and let the puppies crawl over her. Laughing, she picked up each one and held it to her, while the others nipped at her fingers and clothes and whined for attention.

"First I'm going to clean this box," Emily said holding a puppy to her nose. "Then I'll feed you guys."

An hour later Emily's mother and Ben came into the room. The puppies were snuggled up next to one another fast asleep—all except the chubby black pup who lay cradled in Emily's arms.

Emily looked up and smiled. "This is the one. While the other puppies played with each other, she just wanted to be with me. She picked me." Emily scratched the pup behind her velvet-soft ears. The puppy stretched, yawned, and fell back asleep. "I think I'll name her Happy, because I'm so happy to have her."

THE END